dear
Miffy

Also by John Marsden

So Much to Tell You
The Journey
The Great Gatenby
Staying Alive in Year 5
Out of Time
Letters from the Inside
Take My Word for It
Looking for Trouble
Tomorrow . . . (Ed.)
Cool School
Creep Street
Checkers
For Weddings and a Funeral (Ed.)
This I Believe (Ed.)
Dear Miffy
Prayer for the 21st Century
Everything I Know About Writing
Secret Men's Business
The *Tomorrow* Series 1999 Diary
The Rabbits
Norton's Hut
Marsden on Marsden
Winter
The Head Book
The Boy You Brought Home
The Magic Rainforest
Millie
A Roomful of Magic

The *Tomorrow* Series
Tomorrow, When the War Began
The Dead of the Night
The Third Day, the Frost
Darkness, Be My Friend
Burning for Revenge
The Night is for Hunting
The Other Side of Dawn

The Ellie Chronicles
While I Live
Incurable
Circle of Flight

dear
Miffy

John Marsden

PAN
Pan Macmillan Australia

John Marsden's website can be visited at
www.johnmarsden.com.au

First published 1997 in Macmillan by Pan Macmillan Australia Pty Limited
This Pan edition published 2007 by Pan Macmillan Australia Pty Limited
1 Market Street, Sydney

National Library of Australia
Cataloguing-in-Publication data:

Marsden, John, 1950-.
Dear Miffy.

For secondary school aged children.
ISBN 978 0 330 42365 6 (pbk).

1. Letters – Juvenile fiction. 2. Love – Juvenile fiction.
3. Teenagers – Juvenile fiction. 4. Young adult fiction.
I. Title.

A823.3

Typeset in 11/15 Sabon by Post Pre-press Group
Printed in Australia by McPherson's Printing Group

Papers used by Pan Macmillan Australia Pty Ltd are natural, recyclable
products made from wood grown in sustainable forests. The manufacturing
processes conform to the environmental regulations of the country of origin.

For Rob Alexander,
may you have
many happy endings

Many, many thanks to Sarah Bower

Dear Miffy,

This is pretty weird—I just suddenly felt like writing to you, don't know why. Suddenly wanted to talk to you, got this strange feeling. It's not like I never think of you. It's the opposite. I think of you every day, every hour. Sometimes more than that even. Things change though, don't they Miff? We both know that. WHAM! Makes me kind of nervous if you really want to know.

I look over my shoulder a lot now. Never used to do that, hey? Remember when I did my balancing act on that concrete wall above the freeway? Good trick, hey? Makes me sweat thinking about it. I can't believe I did that. Give me a million bucks right now and I still wouldn't do it, couldn't anyway, so what's the use?

You know where I am right now, Miffy? I guess you wouldn't. I'm in the back of the TV room. I'm watching the others while they watch the movie. To tell you the truth, that's what gave me the idea of writing to you. The movie—I don't even know its name—that's what set me off thinking about you and me again. See, in the movie, it was just like us. It's crap, but it's just like us. This boy meets this girl at school see, when they're both in trouble with the

Principal. They're outside his office waiting to see him. They're there for two different things but—she's got an 'attitude problem', he's been nicking off from school.

'Attitude problem.' Doesn't that crack you up? I love it how they call it an 'attitude problem' just because you don't want to spend the best years of your life sitting in a straight line, talking in a straight line, walking in a straight line. Just because you don't want to do what they want you to do. And then they try to tell you that you're the one who's sick.

I don't think so.

Anyway.

So, back to the movie, there they are sitting outside the office waiting to see the Principal and of course they start talking and little sparkles come out of their mouth and away they go . . . like, love at first sight and all that crap.

OK, I know the last part's not like us, but how about that first bit, hey?

I thought you were such a stuck-up bitch, Miffy. I thought you were bloody good looking, I admit that, but I thought you were that stuck-up I didn't care what you looked like.

You know the first words you said to me? Ever? I asked you once and you couldn't remember. But geez, I remember.

It was outside Hammond's office that day, of course. I tried to get in between you and his door, so I could go first, and I was being all polite to you and I said, 'Hey, do you mind if I go in first cos I've got to see Fishbum after this,' and you said, 'Hey, do you mind if I shove my docs up your arse?'

Nice! Before I could think of anything to say back, the door opened and Hammond was standing there saying, 'Well, well, well, all the usual suspects. And Miss Simmons, you've come along to make up the numbers, I suppose.'

Sarcastic bastard.

You gave him a note and he read it and then he said to you: 'Who was the boy involved?' and you said, 'Nick Tremayne,' and he said, 'I should have guessed,' then he said to Mrs McVeigh, 'Right, get Nick Tremayne from 10W, would you please?' and he went back into his office and shut the door and I said to you, 'You lagging bitch,' because Nick was a mate of mine in those days, then you picked up the Rock Eisteddfod trophy and hit me across the head with it, as hard as you could.

Geez, it bloody hurt. I didn't see it coming till too late, so I didn't get my hand up fast enough, otherwise I would have stopped it. The next thing I'm against the wall trying not to fall over and there's blood

pouring down my face and when I realise
what's happened I try to get across to where
you are because I want to kill you, that's all
I want to do, but Mrs McVeigh's screaming
and Hammond and Fishbum and even
Paspaley are all pouring out of their offices,
so I've got as much chance as a stray cat at
KFC.

Anyway they had to call my aunt and I
had to go down to the hospital and get my
head X-rayed and I got a day off, so that
was cool. You got a week off, suspension,
good one, hey? Must have been a big thrill
for your parents.

I was waiting for you to get back so I
could beat the total crap out of you, but
before you did, Nick told me the full story:
how you'd all agreed Nick'd take the rap so
Sam and Georgie and Dino wouldn't get
busted. So that left me up the creek a bit.

I still had a go at you but, in the gym,
and I know you remember that. You were
coming out as I was going in and I took a
look around to make sure no teachers were
watching, then I got you up against the wall
and said, 'Listen you moll, touch me again
and I'll kick your fucking head in.'

You just looked at me like I was some
scum that had overflowed out of the
sewerage. Then I heard Ellis' door open so
I had to let you go.

They were our first two dates. Pretty good, hey?

Love at first sight? I don't think so.

I'm being hassled to go to bed so I'd better stop. I don't want them to read this, that's the main thing.

See ya,

Tony

Dear Miff,

Hey, it wasn't bad writing that letter to you last night. Never written so much in my life. Pretty weird, hey? But I don't care.

Yeah, so only problem now is I want to do another one but I don't know what to write about.

Oh well, might just keep doing the same as last night, raving on about us and school and all that.

Geez, we carried on like dickheads for a while, hey. Nick called it the 'hate stare'— the way we'd give each other greasies. I don't know how it happened. How can you hate someone you've only spoken about six words to? I hated you, but. And you sure hated me. Everything you did, I hated. I'd look at you and just think everything about

5

you was totally off. If you didn't wash your hair I'd think it was woggy. If you wore make-up I'd think you were up yourself, and if you didn't I'd think you looked like a corpse. When you wore that black jacket, I'd say you were too good for us, and when you wore your old jeans I'd say you looked like a moll. If you answered a teacher's question I'd say you were sucking up and if you didn't I'd say you were dumb.

Everyone knew we hated each other and it was kind of a joke to them, but not to me it wasn't. Not to you, either.

Then Nick had that party. 'What do you want to invite her for?' that's what I said to him when I found out you were coming.

'Oh, you know mate, I owe her one,' he said.

'What for?'

I'd already forgotten all the stuff about him and Sam and Georgie and Dino, and how they would have got busted if you hadn't worked out that bullshit story for Hammond. But Nick hadn't forgotten.

'Oh shit, mate, she saved Georgie's ass, she's pretty smart. Georgie thought I was a legend after that, mate. She would have got suspended if I hadn't taken the rap for her. That's how I got my end in, mate.'

I'd heard that last part of the story about fifteen times.

But Miffy, you know what I couldn't work out: why'd you hate me? I mean, I know why I hated you, because I thought you were a snob, a rich bitch—and because you floored me with the Rock Eisteddfod trophy and made me look like an idiot in front of the other kids. You never would tell me why you hated me, but I reckon it was my reputation. I reckon you believed all that shit that people said about me. When I tried to talk to you about it you'd change the subject, but I still reckon you believed it.

So now I'll tell you the truth, Miffy, and one thing's for sure, you can't shut me up in a letter.

OK, when I was twelve my family busted up. Oh yeah, you knew that. My mum, I didn't know where she'd gone. She just pissed off when I was at school one day. Never heard from her no more. Anyway, I didn't care where she went; I didn't care if I never saw her again, still don't. Then all that shit happened with my little brother and about a month after that my father went to Queensland to look for a job, and somewhere for both of us to live. I moved in with my uncle and aunt. But the trouble was, seemed like my dad was taking a long time to find a place where I could come and stay with him. He'd ring up every week or two and I'd be on the phone crying my little eyes out and begging him to let me come up there and he'd get mad and tell me to put my uncle on. Then, after he'd hung up, my uncle and aunt'd get mad at me for upsetting him. So seemed like I just couldn't win.

Then one night my dad rang again and talked to my uncle and this time I wasn't even allowed to talk to him. And when my uncle got off the phone he said my father got a job on a fishing boat and I wouldn't be able to live with him at all. Then that night, when I was in bed, I heard them talking, my uncle and aunt I mean, and they were arguing, and I heard my aunt saying, 'Well, we don't want him either,' and my uncle said, 'I don't know what she's got against kids anyway, but we're stuck with him unless Jim comes to his bloody senses,' and my aunt said, 'Who is she anyway, the same one or another one?' and my uncle said, 'The same one, of course, he's not that bad,' and my aunt said, 'Oh, isn't he just. Well, in my book, a man who walks out on his kid as soon as some bit of skirt comes along isn't much good to anyone,' and my uncle said, 'Well, what about Rosie then?' and my aunt said, 'She's just as bad—no, worse. I still think it's a woman's job, I don't care what anyone says, and what happened to Owen is all her fault as far as I'm concerned.'

So I knew it all then, or I thought I did. Anyway I knew my father didn't want me because he'd found a girlfriend. And you can bet I was pretty upset. But I didn't show my feelings to anyone: I think that's when I first started covering stuff up; I just decided it was better that way. They try and teach you here that it's not, that it's better to talk about stuff, but I'm still getting an *F* in that.

Oh well, life went on, for about three months. Then one day I was down the markets helping this friend of mine, Salvatore, you don't know him, he goes to St Bernard's, and his father's got a stall at the markets.

And I seen my father.

At first I thought, 'Oh good, he's back from Queensland at last and he's looking for me, about bloody time,' and I was going to go racing over there, but something, I don't know what, made me pause for a sec. And then I realised he was with someone, this tall chick with red hair and kind of leopard-skin pants like that lady on TV, and what's more he didn't look like he was in a hurry to find no-one, and neither did she. And then I thought, 'How would he know I was here, anyway?' because not even my uncle and aunt knew: they were still in bed when I left and I just said I was going to a mate's, could have been anyone. They didn't even know Salvatore. So I was standing there spinning out, thinking about all this, and next thing they're right at the stall and they still haven't seen me. And me dad and this chick are all lovey-dovey holding hands and shit and he asks something about the apples and Sal's dad says, 'Did you like those Rome Beauties I got you *last week*?' Last fucking week! And at that minute me dad looks up and sees me and I say, 'You've been back from Queensland a week!' and he looks guilty as hell and suddenly I realise and I say, 'You never even went to fucking Queensland!' and before I know what I'm doing I've picked up a knife off the fruit stall and rammed it right into the chick. I would have stuck it into me dad only she was closer. It was weird, but Miff, it went in so easy, I didn't mean it to go in that far, I swear, I just meant to, you know, nick her a bit, scare everyone. And suddenly this bitch is screaming her fucking head off and she's fallen down on the ground and there's blood just leaking out of her and it won't stop and my dad goes down to help her but he just falls over. I didn't work out for a long time that he'd fainted, a lot of use to everyone. But other people, Sal's mum especially, she's there and she done a good job. Then suddenly there's people everywhere. No-one notices me for a bit, I've dropped the knife and I'm standing there thinking, Oh shit, what have I done? What did I do that for? Then this bloke from the next stall grabs me like I'm a dangerous criminal or something. It's funny, I didn't feel dangerous. Anyway, I just stand there and let him hold me till the cops come, even though Sal's dad keeps saying, 'It's all right, you don't have to hold him, he's a good boy,' though I don't know how he'd worked that out, cos he hardly knew me.

I was spinning out, man; really spinning out.

So the ambulance comes and the cops come and it's like something out of TV only it's real.

Weird, Miff; really weird.

Well, anyway, that's what happened.

Hey, that party of Nick's, it was pretty funny when you think about it, although it didn't seem that way at the time.

Geez, we went for it, didn't we? I've never had such a full-on fight with a girl before. You were pretty crazy doing that with me, considering my reputation. You had guts, Miff, got to give you credit. I don't know how pissed you were, but.

I know I was pissed out of my brain.

I still beat you pretty easy though, hey?
Sorry about the scar. But I've still got the
scar on the back of my neck. I thought it
would have gone by now, but hey, maybe
it's a permanent one, reminder of you.

Shit, look how much I've written. I must
be crazy. Stuff this for a joke, I'm going to
bed.

See ya around,

T o n y

Dear Miff,

I don't know how I got so fucking
violent, Miff. Do you know? You probably
do, you're so fucking smart. But you were
pretty violent yourself. At first, anyway. I
just can't seem to help myself, Miff. I wish
you were here so I could talk to you about
stuff. These letters, they're crazy, hey, but
I'm still writing them.

Every time we met, for about two or
three months, there was hatred in the air.
No love in the air for us, hey. Remember
when I pulled that chair out from under
you and you nearly broke your back? I did
get scared that time. See I was on probation
from the court and probation from the

school and on a contract with my uncle and aunt and I thought I'd blown the whole lot in one hit. I was more scared about that than about making you a paraplegic for life, if you want to know the truth. That's the kind of selfish bastard I was. And maybe still am. I don't know. Sometimes I think I've changed and I'm better; sometimes I think I'm worse.

But even that day, standing there watching you on the floor with everyone thinking you'd wrecked your back and me thinking I was going to be put in care for the next five years, I still didn't give a flicker. Not a flicker. Tough guy, big man, that's me.

Come to think of it, you were pretty tough yourself—I was kind of shocked that you didn't cry. Impressed, but I hated you for it as well. I think I wanted to make you cry or something. It's not like I had this conscious thought that I wanted to do it, but when I looked at you I just seemed to want to make you cry. I can't explain it any better than that.

Geez, I said some terrible things to you for a few months there. In Maths that day when you said something and I said, 'Hey, if I'd wanted to hear from an arsehole I would have farted.'

Pretty good line, hey? Not original

though. Wish it was. Wish I had thought of it myself.

I never could figure you out, Miff, not for a long time. Maybe never at all when I think about it. It was just with you being so rich and all. No, more than that. Other kids at school were rich. But they were rich without much class. You were rich and you had class. Like, the way you said stuff. You never said 'youse' or 'shut up' or 'g'day' or stuff like that. I couldn't work out what you were doing in our school. You didn't seem to belong. The clothes you had, even your jewellery, it was just different to what I was used to. We're all moccas and tats and shit, you know what I mean, but I had the feeling you wouldn't have any fluffy dice in your car. Then Georgie told me how you'd been chucked out from some big richo private school. I got pretty interested then. But no-one could tell me why you got chucked out. I was trying everything to find the reason. Then Dino said, 'How come you keep asking about her—do you like her or something?' and I said, 'No way, mate,' so I didn't ask any more then, cos you know what they're like—they get their teeth into an idea like that and they're worse than vampires with virgins, they never let go. So I shut up fast.

But I'll tell you what I did. I never told

you this before. I followed you home. I was like a stalker! I felt pretty weird about it, but I just had to know more about your life. I followed you to the station and waited till you'd gone down to one end of the platform, then I went up to the other end. And when you got off at Kramer I mixed in with the crowd and kept about a hundred metres behind as you went down Ferris Avenue. You went left at St Peter's Street—well, I don't need to tell you cos I guess you know the way to your own house—and it got tricky then cos it's such a quiet street. I had to stay way, way back. I was worried you'd go into some house and I wouldn't even be able to see which one. Then you crossed the road to Moriah Place. As soon as you'd gone I ran over there. Must have looked bloody suss to anyone who was watching. Luckily, I don't think anyone was. I was just in time to see you going into this mansion. I thought, 'Geez, unbelievable.' I mean, fair dinks, Miff: I'd only seen places like yours on TV. I thought it must have been about a hundred years old, your house, all that ivy and stuff. All white and big and them green shutters, and the garden out the front with them roses and all that other shit. And the tennis court. I mean, fuck.

I couldn't get that close because I was

scared you'd see me, but I got a good-enough view. I watched for about ten minutes, then this lady came along with her dog and she looked at me like I was a used condom and the dog growled at me like I was a kilo of steak, so I thought I'd better rack off.

But I hated you even worse after that. Just, I don't know, not exactly because you were rich. Because you seemed like you had everything, I guess. I felt like I had nothing and you had it all. I tried to imagine what it'd be like living in a place like that and I couldn't even start. It's like you're trying to tune a radio and you can't even find a station. I felt sick every time I thought about you inside that big house.

That's when we had that fight at PE. You remember? We were doing netball and I got this bib saying *WA* and you said, 'What's that stand for: wanker?' and you had one with a *C*. I said, 'What's that stand for: cunt?' and you chucked the ball at me and then tried to rip my face off. I won that fight, too—or at least I was winning it until Ellis broke it up.

That was the first time we got sent to Hammond together, like for the same offence. We sat there in the corridor, steam coming out of our ears. Hammond made us shake hands! Can you believe it? What a dickhead. Then that big speech about my being on probation and shit. I don't reckon he had a right to say so much in front of you. It was none of your business.

Then, when we got outside, you said, 'What are you on probation for?' and I said, 'None of your fucking business.' I just couldn't believe what was happening, that Hammond had opened up my life to you like that. Like, you'd tried to rip my face off and failed, and then he comes along and kind of rips it off anyway. You know what I mean? All the stuff he said about me, a lot of that was real private. I'm getting mad all over again thinking about it now. 'I know your mother leaving so suddenly like that, and then what happened with your brother, these things have been difficult for you to deal with.' He was saying stuff like that. Fuck him. I couldn't believe I was hearing it. If I hadn't been in so much trouble already I would have gone him, I reckon. But what hope have you got? You can't beat those blokes.

Another thing that really got me, I couldn't figure how anyone living in your kind of house could have any idea about my life. I thought I must have been a Martian to you. It never crossed my mind that you'd care about someone like me. So that's why I told you to fuck off.

Sorry.

Anyway, fuck this letter, too. I've had enough of this writing shit. Might give it the ass I think.

Nightie-night, Miff.

Tony

Dear Miff,

Geez, I feel like shit tonight, Miff. I mean everything's shit these days but some days are worse than others and this is bad, bad, bad.

Seems like the nights are the worst times.

How does it all work, Miff? I don't understand it at all, not one little bit.

There's fuck all to do at this place. Like, there's a pool table, nothing else. And that's pretty hacked from blokes stuffing around with it. The computer's totally hacked. I've got my CD but the batteries have had it, and you're not allowed to use the things, what do you call them, those three little holes in the wall where you plug stuff in? I mean, people do, but you just get in more trouble.

I was thinking about my uncle and aunt,

you know. I don't even know where they are any more. I don't care a helluva lot either, but that's another matter. After the stabbing they went apeshit. You can't blame them for that, of course. But it's not like I killed her or anything. You'd think I had, the way they turned it on. My uncle, when they bailed me, he took me back to their place and beat the crap out of me. I mean, full on. I knew I couldn't fight back, I just had to take it. I mean, he'd been a boxer, you know. Did I ever tell you that? Twenty-eight fights, fifteen wins, two draws, two disqualifications, nine losses. He got knocked out six times. Like, that's a lot of knock-outs. I reckon it fucked him up a bit, fucked his brain up, but you reckon I'd ever say that to him?

He really could punch. I had to go back to the cop shop for an interview the next day and I had bruises all over. My head was the size of a watermelon. The cop said, 'Been in another fight, have you?' and I just said, 'Yeah' and he didn't say nothing, he knew, he just looked at my uncle and my uncle didn't say nothing neither, just sat there looking at the wall, and the cop said, 'You ought to be more careful,' but I don't know who he was talking to, me or me uncle. Cos me uncle, he had a few mates in the force, he knew quite a lot of them.

Bastards.

It's not like they were real bad, my uncle and aunt, I'm not saying that. I mean you've got to see it from their point of view. They never had no kids of their own, and it's not like they wanted to and couldn't, like some people: it's because they didn't want any. And then suddenly along comes this kid who gets shoved on them just because his old man wants to go off and fuck some young chick. And I know I'm not that easy to get on with. Like, I know some of the stuff I do really shits some people. I know that. They didn't like my music, and the stuff I wanted to watch on TV, not that I'm into TV much, but sometimes there'd be something good, like that 'Rats Unplugged' concert.

They didn't like the stuff I did to my hair, and the rings and shit, and some of my mates, Nick and Ali for instance, they didn't think much of them, neither. For a while they banned my mates from the house. If my mates came around they had to stay outside, like, I had to go and talk to them out in the street. Good one, hey? Did a real lot for my social life.

Then, after the stabbing, I was grounded something bad. I couldn't see why really. I mean, it's not like I was some uncontrollable maniac who was going to go

around the streets killing people. I only
stabbed her cos of me dad and all that.
I just lost my head. Before that I'd been on
a curfew of nine o'clock school nights, and
midnight weekends, which was pretty
bloody stupid, but after the stabbing I was
on a curfew of nothing! I had to come
straight home after school and I wasn't
allowed out at all. Even to go to the bloody
shops I had to get down on my knees and
beg. It was like, what do they call it, house
arrest. It wasn't that good an idea for them
anyway, because it meant I was there all the
time. Every time they turned around, there
I was. In the kitchen, in the yard, in the
lounge with the TV turned up real loud.
I was doing it half-deliberately, you know,
cos I figured they'd soon get jack of it, get
jack of me, but I think I got jack of them
before they got jack of me.

Anyway, you know what adults are like,
they couldn't keep it up for ever. I wore
them down after a while. We had some
terrible fights first, but. They still wouldn't
let me go to parties but I could go to
friends' houses, or down the shops, or to
the footy. Well, that's where I said I was
going. I think footy's pretty boring if you
want to know the truth, but it was a good
excuse to get out of the place.

That's when I started hanging around

with Franco so much. His mum let him do whatever he wanted. She never had no control over him. And he always had heaps of money so he could buy them little placcie bags. You know what I'm talking about. I don't want to say too much here in case these bastards read it. They want to know everything. But yeah, Franco, he was good that way. I kept saying, 'I'll pay you back, Franco, I swear I will,' and he'd just say, 'Don't worry about it, I don't give a shit.' I never got into no heavy stuff, not really, but geez, I gave that soft shit a hell of a workout.

Franco, he wasn't that popular, but when I started hanging around with him he got accepted better. So he thought that was all right.

Anyway, you don't want to hear all this, Miff. It's ancient history now, hey?

So, be seeing you (joke).

T o n y

Hi Miff,

How's things where you are? I wonder how you're getting on, and where you are, I really do.

I'd like to visit you, Miff; I'd like it very much.

That first day you took me to your place, I was trying so hard to be cool. I bet you knew that. Well, I kind of gave it away when I said I wouldn't go unless it was just us two, I didn't want to be there with your parents or anyone, couldn't have handled that. But I was still packing shit. It was sort of funny, because I had to pretend I didn't know the way, never seen it before etc, etc. Suddenly there I was, going along the yellow brick road, through the magical gates into the golden palace and, even though you'd told me all that terrible stuff about your father, I put it in the back of my mind, because I convinced myself that living in a house like that would have to be like living in fucking Beverly Hills, just everything beautiful, blokes in white coats handing out drinks from silver trays, everyone sitting around having little chats about the fucking opera or something.

What did get me, though—and what I'll never forget—is how cold everything was. It was weird to me. I'd never been in a house like yours, Miff. Everything was so, you know, like a shop or something. I was trying to count the number of TVs, but I don't know how many there were. That one in the lounge, that was about the size of a movie screen. And everything looked so expensive. I reckon stuff like the rug in front of your fireplace would have cost more than all the furniture in my uncle and aunt's place put together.

All those old pictures on the walls with their little lights above them like the place we went to on the Art excursion, geez, I couldn't believe that.

I kept thinking, geez, it's a wonder no-one's ever done a burg here.

Yeah, no risk about it Miff, your family had the big bucks.

But a lot of the stuff was fake, too. Like, the house itself. I thought it was really old but when we got close you told me it was built seven years ago and just made to look old. Those plants in the first room: when you opened the front door they looked great, but they were all artificial. You couldn't hardly tell, but. Then there were the walls. I thought that shit was painted on them, but when you get up close it was only wallpaper. The fire was burning away like there was proper logs in the bastard but it was only gas! Sometimes it seemed like nothing in the house was for fucking real.

You were showing me all this stuff and I was just going, 'Oh yeah, right, seen that. OK, what's in the next room?'

I didn't want to give you the satisfaction.

We went upstairs, walking on that carpet. It was like walking on feathers. More paintings on the walls. You know which one I liked but, don't you? That great big one with the clouds all rolled back and the angels and shit. Pretty corny, but who cares? Whatever turns you on, I reckon.

Well, I know what really turned me on, and that was you in your bedroom. Don't think I'll write about that, but; I don't want to cream me PJs, I got a clean pair on tonight. I'll write about your bedroom instead. Pretty nice room, Miff! Good views. Geez, you can see the city and right across to the bay. And it's so big, your room I mean. When I was going out with Becky I spent a bit of time in her room, just an hour or two here and there, don't get the wrong idea, but it was kind of different to yours. She had magazine pictures stuck on her walls, and cheap old furniture that rocked every time you touched it, and perfume that smelled like that plastic shit you hang up in toilets. She had a mirror that was all blotchy and the ceiling was fuzzy with mould and the bed was so soft in the middle it was like sleeping in a sponge.

Not that I'd know what the bed was like, of course.

Your room, everything in it matched, that's what got me. Like, the flowers on the wallpaper matched the leaves on the doona, and the gold in the carpet matched the edges of the doona and the curtains, just everything matched.

I'll say one thing for myself, Miff, I'm observant. I notice all that stuff. I even noticed how the clock had those little rose things twirling around it. I mean, it was all kind of square, old-fashioned, but geez it was nice, Miff. It got to be my favourite place in all the world, the only place where I felt a bit of peace, you know what I mean?

Bloody different from my bedroom here.

You know, sometimes I wish we'd gotten on with each other a lot earlier, because then I would have been able to spend more time with you. We only had three months when we got on, a bit less really, and four months fighting. I wish it had been the other way around, at least. Geez, we wasted those four months, didn't we? Ripping into each other. I didn't understand you then. I didn't try to understand you. It took me a long time to figure out what the deal was with you and why you were the way you were. Pretty dumb, hey? But you didn't give me a lot of help. You didn't give anyone a lot of help.

I thought you were just too big a snob to bother with scum like me.

See, everyone thought I was scum, Miff—at least they treated me like they did. Just everyone. Geez, I'm getting sorry for myself now, but I can't help it. As long as I don't cry. You don't cry in here. I just felt like everyone was putting shit on me, every chance they got. My uncle and aunt, it's like they just waited for me to make a mistake. It was like they wanted me to make mistakes. Didn't matter what it was—a drip of tomato sauce on the floor, getting in late from a movie, a pack of ciggies in my pocket. They were out to bust me. It was like living with a couple of cops, I reckon.

And speaking of cops, the pigs were out to put shit on me, too. Geez, they made it hard. Like, before I did that terrible thing to me dad's girlfriend they'd pulled me up a few times. After that but, when I was on bail, they must have all known me then, because once my uncle and aunt let me go out again the cops stopped me every bloody day. Well, just about. Fair dinkum, it was no joke. They never beat up on me or nothing, like they've done to some of me mates, but they just hassle you. And they try to scare you. They make all these threats about how they're going to get you. And how they're going to make sure you get put away and how you're going to get the shit beaten out of you, and raped and stuff, once you're in there. And there's no way I was gonna let them know they were getting to me, but they were.

So I was getting it on the streets, getting it at my uncle and aunt's, and if that wasn't enough, I was getting it at school, from the teachers. And, geez, was I getting it there. Once they heard about me getting charged, I was like the worst mother-fucker in the whole place. Hammond, I reckon he followed me round the school trying to pick me. Funny though, the worst stuff wasn't him giving me dets and sending letters home and putting me on report and stuff. The worst thing was the bullshit he kept hanging on me about what a failure I was. You know, 'Great future for you, Tony, you'll be in jail by the time you're eighteen,' 'You've got no hope, son—you tell me what kind of employer'd take someone like you.'

I suppose they all talk like that but it just eats at you somehow, even though you know it's bullshit and they wouldn't know if their arses were on fire. I reckon the girls are better off—they get counselling and shit from teachers when they're mucking up. Even the girls say that they can get the teachers on the end of a string, especially the men. Dirty buggers, they still reckon they can pull some sixteen-year-old chick by talking to her about her problems.

It wasn't just Hammond, though. It was Fishburn or Fishbum or whatever his name is. He'd look at me and shake his head like I was some hopeless case.

They're all the fucking same, teachers, I reckon.

I don't want to think about them fuckheads anyway.

I don't know, seems like I can't work anything out at the moment.

I was thinking again tonight about stabbing that bitch at the markets, Miff. Seems unbelievable, don't it? Like, one minute I'm a typical teenager with all the typical teenage problems, worst thing I ever done just about was racking stuff from shops with Nick (hey, good name for doing that, Nick, what do you reckon?) plus one night I went for a spin with Dougie in a very hot Calais, like very hot, so hot that if they'd caught us I'd have got third-degree burns. But I swear, that was the worst thing I'd ever done. And then the next minute I'm a psycho. You know what I mean? I'm the same bloke, same bloke the day before the stabbing as I was the day after, but everything was different . . .

Oh, geez, I don't know, I don't know what I'm saying, cos everything changes you, doesn't it? So when I put that knife into her, I know it did change me. But I mean, fuckit, everything changes you. You have a Quarter Pounder instead of a Big Mac, it changes you. You cross the street at the lights instead of fifty metres along, it changes you. Turn left instead of right, sit at this desk instead of that one, say 'Yes' instead of 'No', watch 'The Larry Freeman Show' instead of 'Whispers', you're different every time and, what's worse, you don't know what you would have been like if you'd done it the other way.

I mean, I know stabbing that lady, it wasn't some little thing like having a Quarter Pounder. I know it was a real big thing. I gotta admit I didn't really know that when I went up before the magistrate, though I said I did, I said I understood the seriousness of it and all that shit. You gotta say that. Geez, you'd be a dickhead if you didn't. Hey, imagine if you stood up in front of the magistrate and said, 'Aw, gee, your worship I dunno what's so bad about sticking a knife in someone; I mean, what's the big deal?'

But, to tell you the truth, I don't really know what it did to her. No-one ever seemed to mention her. It was like she was a banned topic. No-one wanted to talk about it. All I know is when me case came up, the police bloke—the prosecutor—said she'd recovered from it physically but she was traumatised by it and getting counselling.

'Traumatised.' Hey, lucky this thing's got spellcheck. Hasn't got 'fuck' in it, but; I checked just a minute ago. Bit of a poor effort, that.

Anyway, like I say, I don't know what it did to her, but I know what it did to me. Fucked me right up. That's why it's all ended like this, I reckon. None of this would have happened. I went from being a naughty boy to being a fucking juvenile fucking delinquent.

Gonna stop now, Miff, before I get fucking RSI or whatever it's called. Don't think that's on spellcheck, either.

Night, Miff.

Tony

Dear Miff,

I'm totally off my head tonight, Miff. Nothing new about that, I suppose. It's just this place, being the way I am now, being here with so many dickheads . . .

One of these guys got busted last night

with half an ounce inside his pillow. I wish I
had a mattress full so I could get totally and
utterly stoned for months to come.

I wish I could hurry up and get through
this sickness that they call life.

Miff, I was thinking about you so much
today, all afternoon. I wish I could see you
and touch you again. Tell you the truth I
want to make love to you, Miff. I know
I can't, but try telling my body that. Your
long black hair, Miff, like poetry: I want to
run my fingers through it. I want to feel its
softness. I want to take a handful of it and
let it fall away strand by strand while I rub
it against my cheek. I want to tap on your
perfect teeth like they're piano keys and I'm
playing a little tune on them—remember
how I did that one time and you laughed
and pushed me away with the lightest touch
I've ever felt?

That was good that day.

Miff, I want to see your breasts again.
You had the most beautiful breasts I've ever
seen. It was like God made them out of
sand, golden sand that was lying in the sun
a thousand years. They were so warm and
alive and firm. When I touched them I
thought my brain was going to melt. I felt
like I'd stop breathing. I could hardly keep
my stuff in me, just from touching them.
The brown buttons, pointing away from

each other, so proud, like little volcanoes: only I was the one going to erupt.

There's this old blues singer, Robert Johnson, so old he's dead, and he sings this song 'Travelling Riverside Blues', and it's got this line in it, 'You can squeeze my lemon, baby, juice runs down my legs.'

Well, you sure squeezed my lemon, Miff, and the juice ran down my legs.

Christ, I love chicks. I know why God invented them: to drive guys mad. I could never be gay, I just love chicks too much.

I'm driving myself mad, writing this, but I can't stop.

Sometimes you did seem about a thousand years old. I felt like an idiot, a clumsy idiot, lying next to you. You seemed so, I don't know, wise, ancient or something, like there was this blood flowing in you and it had been flowing through chicks since the beginning of time. It gave you this understanding of stuff that I knew I'd never have. Doesn't matter how long I live, I'll never have that.

'Can't you hear me howling, baby, down on my bended knees?' That's Robert Johnson again. Different song, but.

The thing is, when I write like this, it's like I'm dreaming onto paper, I can escape into that past world where I used to live, and even though at the time a lot of it

sucked bad, really bad, when I go back and
live in it like I'm doing now, it don't seem
so shitty after all. You know one thing, it's
a whole lot better than what I've got now.
I don't want to think about what I've got
now, so instead of thinking about it I write
these letters to you. And then I feel better.
Makes sense, don't it? Pretty smart, you got
to admit. And they used to reckon I was so
dumb at school.

Sex, I can't stop thinking about it, but.
It's like the best sweetest torture ever
invented. It tears you apart but you
wouldn't want it any other way. It's the
drug you never try to give up. It's the
poison that flows through your system and
you'd rather have it than food or drink or
dope because it makes you feel SO
FUCKING GREAT! Even while it makes
you depressed.

Thank you, God, for inventing sex. You
did us all a big favour.

Thank you, Miff, for the great sex. It
was fantastic, even if sometimes it wasn't as
good as it was at other times, if you know
what I mean, and I think you would. But
even bad sex is better than no sex.

This is doing me no good, Miff, no good
at all. I was wrong what I said before,
about how great it is writing these letters.
How it makes me feel better. It doesn't

make me feel better. It makes me feel like all I want to do is die. And I can't even do that. Remember how Mr Ellis reckoned there was this Japanese soldier in World War Two and he was captured and that was like a big disgrace for him and he tried to kill himself but they tied his hands so he couldn't? What he did was, he just lay down in the bottom of the boat and willed himself to die. And he did. Like, he thought himself to death. Don't reckon I could do that, but. So I'll just go to bed like I do every night—every fucking boring night— and go into my dreaming death instead. And think about how I'll probably never have sex with anyone except myself again.

Bye.

T o n y

D e a r   M i f f ,

Don't want to think about what I wrote last night, Miff. I got a feeling it was pretty bloody dumb.

I dreamed about you again, but; like I do most nights. Sometimes it's nightmares, sometimes it's good dreams, sometimes I have to change the sheets. Depends on whether I'm remembering the beginning or the middle or the end, don't it? Geez, for a long time I didn't think there was going to be a middle or an end. It was pretty amazing that we ever got together, wasn't it? When you think about how we started. And it was funny the way it happened. I like thinking about that day. That's the best part of going with anyone, I reckon: the first time when you realise you like each other, that she feels the same way you do, and it's like, 'Fuck! This is magic!'

Still, with us it was just a bloody shock. I didn't know you liked me and I sure as hell didn't know I liked you! And it was exactly the same for you!

Geez, that day, I'll never forget it.

At first it was just bloody embarrassing. When I got to the det and realised it was only us two, no-one else, all I could think of was this movie I saw yonks ago where some bunch of high school kids get a Saturday morning det and they talk about life and stuff as if they're real good buddies.

All these movies, a lot of them seem like us, don't you reckon?

But when I was thinking about that *Breakfast Club* movie I was just laughing, thinking nothing like that could ever happen with us.

I didn't even know anyone else had a

det; I thought it was a little treat Fishbum had dreamed up especially for me. I can see his point, but: if he's going to waste his Saturday at school he might as well get even with everyone he can think of. Why keep it just for me?

So there it was. I rolled up ten minutes late, feeling pretty proud of myself that I'd got out of bed at all. And there you were, walking up to the door at exactly the same moment.

'What the fuck are you doing here?' I said. It was the most polite I'd ever been to you, but I got such a shock to see you, that's why.

'I've got a fucking det with fucking Fishbum,' you said. You flicked your hair out of your eyes. Your hair was still wet; I guess you'd washed it and then had to hurry to get to school. But I always remember how beautiful you looked as you flicked that long wet beautiful black hair. You always walked like a panther anyway, and you had eyes like one, and you never looked more like a panther than you did that morning.

'So have I,' I said. 'I thought I was the only one.'

'I hope we're not the only two,' you said. 'I don't want to spend the next three hours locked in a room with you.'

You seemed different to normal, but.
Kind of . . . switched off. Like you weren't
awake yet, sure, but more than that: like
you had your ropes cut and you were
drifting in some big old sea and you didn't
know the name of it or whether it was
water or what. I felt a bit weird being
around you when you were like that.

Like, even when you were telling me
how you didn't want me in the same room,
you seemed you weren't really thinking
about it. Like, your mind was in another
place.

But before I could say anything Fishbum
appeared. He didn't yell at us for being late,
the way I thought he would. Guess he was
pleased we'd turned up at all. And besides,
Saturday morning is, like, different;
everyone seems kind of quieter. The school
felt pretty weird. Everything echoed, and it
all looked bare and empty.

He just put us in that room, B13 I think
it was, and gave us our work, then off he
went to his own little office. And there we
were for three hours, just the two of us: the
two worst enemies in the southern
hemisphere and no-one else to talk to.

It was pretty cold and silent in there for
a while, hey? You sat on one side of the
room, I sat on the other. We couldn't have
got any further away from each other. I just

stared at the textbook. I would have read the same sentence seventeen times and I still didn't know what the first word was. I always do that, Miff; I don't know whether I'm stupid or what, but I can read a sentence a hundred times and not have a clue what it's about. The words sit there on the page like dead black ants.

So there I was, doing that, with the cold starting at my feet and working its way up my legs.

I think it was about when it reached my knees that I got my big shock.

You were crying.

You, the great Miffy Catriona Simmons, princess of Salmon Heights, ex Warrington Girls' Grammar School, toughest wildest bitch in the school, more vicious than a rattlesnake with rabies, colder than a Maths classroom . . .

And you were crying.

At first I thought you had a cold and your nose was dripping onto the paper. And the sniffling noises were because of your cold. Then I realised what was really happening. I just couldn't believe it. Impossible! I sat there in shock. And before I could stop myself I said, 'You're crying.'

You didn't say anything. And I said, 'What are you crying for?' I was, like, amazed.

And you said, through these little sobs,
'Mind your own fucking business.'

I said, 'OK, I will.'

So we both just kept on sitting there,
you still crying, me still in shock. Then I
saw Fishbum's head coming towards the
room. I said, 'Fishbum's coming.' That gave
you time to wipe your eyes and try and
look normal. He came in and stood next to
you for about five minutes, probably trying
to look down your front, I reckon. He
didn't say anything, but. Then he came over
to my desk and did the same thing, except I
don't think he was trying to look down my
front. Then he went out. He hadn't said a
word, not one.

And there we were, alone, just the two
of us again.

I guess a lot of people who think they
know me don't know me too well. A lot of
people think I'm some total mongrel who
couldn't give a shit about anyone: who'd
pick up a cat and give it the helicopter
treatment on top of a fifty-storey building,
then let it go.

I reckon I'd do that, too. I don't like
cats. And face it, I've done worse.
Remember Clint Eastwood in that movie:
'I've killed just about everything that walks
and crawls, at one time or another.' I've
killed mice and frogs and lizards and birds,

and even a dog once, except that was an accident. But one thing I just can't hack, one thing I can't stand, even for a minute, is seeing a girl cry. It makes me feel so damn bad. I can't sit there and listen to it. So in case you've ever wondered, that's why I tried again after you'd pissed me off so bad the first time.

I think I said something like, 'What the fuck's the big problem anyway?' which I guess didn't sound too sympathetic and you didn't even bother to answer. Which was fair enough. But at the time I didn't think that; I got the shits with you and said, 'You reckon you're so bloody tough and now you're carrying on like a fucking wimp.'

See, I just couldn't stand to see you crying, like I said, so I was saying anything that I thought might shut you up.

Boy, you really cracked then. 'WHAT THE FUCK WOULD YOU KNOW?' That's when you started chucking the books. I was ducking and dodging, and at the same time trying to look out the window to see if Fishbum was coming. I thought, If he comes, we're dead. I was counting on you running out of books. But I guess I must have miscounted because, just as I took one more quick look out the window, you got me fair and square on the side of the head with your fucking mobile phone. Geez, I was pissed off. It wasn't one of those little wussy phones that most people have; no, not this baby: it was a thing called The Brick and it felt like one, too. 'Geez, you're a fucking bitch,' I was going to say, but I couldn't even finish the sentence, because you started crying full-on then, like you were totally out of control. Scary stuff. I went over to where you were sitting and you had your head right down on the desk and I didn't even know if you could tell I was there. I wanted to touch you but I was nervous about it and I had blood running down the side of my face—it was pretty funny, I guess, when you look back on it, but at the time it wasn't.

I thought if I touched you, there was every chance you'd belt me again or else you'd get Fishbum and have me charged with assault or harassment or something. Still, I couldn't help myself. I put out a finger and gave your hair a bit of the old stroke stroke treatment and when you didn't shove your pencil case down my throat I got a bit more daring and went for the shoulder. And next thing you're holding me like I'm your best friend, and you're sobbing all over my shirt.

So that's how it started. Last thing I expected when I went in for the det. I've never had anything good come out of a det before. And it wasn't all good—Fishbum

cracked the shits when he saw how little
work we'd done, and on Monday he
dobbed us in to Paspaley. But I'd been there
and done that enough times before. And
Paspaley's such a weak bastard. I seen him
playing table tennis with the Year 12s and
he was bloody pathetic, doing all these
wussy little shots and they were smashing
the crap out of the ball, smashing it right at
him, and you could see they were doing it
deliberately, and he was giving this weak
little smile, like he wanted to be in on the
joke, and he didn't realise that he was the
joke.

Anyway, I just wanted to write about us,
to make myself feel bad, not about
Paspaley, which *really* makes me feel bad.

Miff, as much as we hated each other
before that det, that's how much we loved
each other after it. Don't you reckon?
I knew I was pretty damn intense about
everything, and now I'd found someone as
intense as me. We walked down the street
to the park and we were just so into each
other.

You know, Miff, touching you was like
eating honey. I had your beautiful hair in
my mouth, your beautiful clean black hair,
and your hands were all down my back,
pressing me so close it was like you wanted
to pull me right into you. You had the

hottest hands I've ever felt, it was like these two hot little animals were running all over me, making me hot wherever they touched. Christ, I wanted to rip my clothes off and your clothes off right there and then, and be right into you, and I know you wanted that too, but being in the middle of a tiny little park, it was a bit difficult. Then, fuck it, you had to go to meet your mother or something, and we had to rip ourselves apart.

Story of my life.

I floated home to my uncle and aunt as if I was on something. And I was, Miff. I was on you. Someone had grabbed a soldering iron and melted us together. Without even having sex we were into each other, like no-one I've ever been with before. It was so wonderful it was scary. So amazingly good that it scared the shit out of me.

I was actually nice to my uncle and aunt for at least half an hour when I got back there. Must have been a helluva shock for them.

You know what they say here, Miff? They say I'm in denial, which I won't bother explaining, and that these letters are all part of the denial. What a lot of shit. They know about the letters by now, of course, cos I spend so much time writing

them, but I don't think they know they're to
you. One thing's for sure, they don't get to
read them. What I do wonder about though
is how they even know they're letters. They
must have been looking over my shoulder
maybe. Makes me kind of nervous.

Anyway, that's enough for now.

See ya.

T o n y

D e a r   M i f f ,

I was saying about being intense and
everything in that last letter, and I've been
thinking about it ever since. It's the way
I am, no risk about that, but geez Miff, I
don't know, it's no good. The trouble is, it
means everything matters so bloody much.
You can't take a joke when you're like me.
Or you. You pretend you can, but you can't
really. That first Monday after we started
going together, I lost it badly when Cam
made that joke about you fucking him for a
Mars Bar. I knew it wasn't true; you've got
too much class to even spit on him, but he's
always giving me the shits, and that day I
went for him. Wham! Bam! Thank you,
Cam. He's the first bloke I've ever knocked

out, like unconscious, with my bare fists,
and I tell you what, it was a bit scary,
I thought I'd killed him for a minute.

He didn't dob on me though, that was
one good thing about him, the only good
thing about him, cos if he'd dobbed, I was
gone, no risk. I was already on so many last
warnings I'd lost count.

I guess everyone was so bloody amazed
that I was with you. That's not surprising,
the way we'd been on Friday, and every day
before that. But they didn't know anything.
They sure as hell didn't know all that stuff
you'd told me on Saturday.

One of the things that meant a helluva
lot to me, Miff, was the way you trusted
me, telling me all that. Trust. Christ, that's a
bloody joke. No-one ever trusted me before.
I swear, I wasn't trusted to wipe my own
bum. My father lying about Queensland,
that was typical. When I was little, every
time I went to the shops for him, he used to
reckon I'd stolen some of his change. He'd
belt me for it if I wasn't quick enough to get
out of his way.

The real joke was that I actually did
steal his change quite often.

But you. You trusted me, Miff. I don't
know why. It could be that you're
incredibly stupid, but I don't think that's it.
You fail all the tests for stupidity that I ever

heard of. Like, I mean you fail them by not being stupid, not the other way round . . . anyway, you know what I mean.

No, I never thought you were stupid, but I've never figured out why you'd pick the biggest delinquent in the whole school, your worst enemy, the kid from such a different bloody world to yours, why you'd tell him stuff you never told anyone else before.

It was a weird experience, believe me. Maybe that's what gave me the feeling I was on something—and for once I wasn't.

So, suddenly I knew so much about you. I felt like I'd walked right inside that big rich house and was sitting in the middle of the big lounge room with the grand piano and the fireplace the size of a garage. Without having met any of the people in the house except you, I knew why your father was so moody and silent, why your grandmother wouldn't speak to him from one week to the next, why your brother and sister only came in to shower and change before they went off for another wild night of sex and drugs and forget about the rock'n'roll.

I always thought doctors were kind of different, you know what I mean? I always thought doctors, with their clean hands and quiet voices and their old-fashioned classy-looking clothes, were like special people who'd been chosen by God or something to be doctors: they didn't have no bad thoughts and they didn't do no bad things. I can't remember who told me your father was a doctor, but I knew from somewhere, and I was a bit nervous about you after I heard it. I thought you must be from another world, like you were an angel, maybe. Is that too weird? Sorry if it is.

Then you told me the whole shithouse story and I was like in shock and excited at the same time. Before that I'd thought there were two worlds, one where people like me lived, a scungy world full of shit where you fought in the gutter just to stay alive, just to score another dollar. Like my mum getting paid about a dollar an hour or some shit to clean rooms in this el cheapo motel with cigarette butts on the carpet and torn flyscreens on the windows. There was good stuff in our world too, like sticking by your mates, but just not enough of that good stuff.

Then—this is what I thought—there was this other world for the rich pigs, where they drove around in their posh BMWs and talked posh to each other and they were all beautiful looking. If they did anything bad it'd be like on TV, where it wouldn't seem really bad, it'd be like glamorous bad, not scungy or shabby or disgusting. I never thought that maybe they could be really rotten underneath.

But your father and that little girl, that was rotten bad, as bad as anything that ever happened in our street, in our suburb. And it was worse in a way, with him paying them off. I'm not saying no-one around here wouldn't pay someone off if they could; the thing is, no-one'd have the money, so it's hypo—whatever that word is—hypothetical, or something.

I don't know what it would do to you, having a pervert for a father. You tried to explain it, a little bit, that day in the det, but we never really talked about it after that. I remember you saying you couldn't stand for him to touch you any more. Geez, I can understand it'd give you the creeps. I don't know how you could even look at him again.

My father had a lot of shit wrong with him but I don't think he'd do anything like that.

I tell you what it did for me: it made me angry as goddamn hell, that's what it did. I seriously thought about ringing the cops and dobbing on him, you know that? Like, anonymously. The only reason I didn't was because I knew how pissed off you'd be.

I had some strange feeling that I was going to be your protector, for God's sake; like, I wanted to take care of you suddenly. You'd have killed me if you'd known that! I don't know anyone who wanted protecting less than you did . . .

Wait a minute though . . .

It's about ten minutes since I wrote the last sentence. I've been thinking about you all that time. And you know, I've just worked out what anyone with an IQ in double figures would have figured out months ago. And it's this: you did want me to look after you! You know what I mean. All that toughness, all that aggro, it was real all right, but geez, you were a kitten when I touched you. A panther with anyone else, but a kitten with me. I never could quite figure that out. I know for sure that no-one else ever saw that side of you. They wouldn't have believed some of the stuff you said when we were just lying together, the way you sometimes went soft and mushy around me. You were like a little kid then. Remember? We used to laugh about it and I'd stir you about needing your dummy and your teddy and stuff, but I kind of liked it when you went that way.

I guess maybe I liked being all protective and shit around you. I don't know, I don't want to think about that.

I'll change the subject.

Well, sort of. The subject's always you, Miff, as far as I'm concerned. I know you wouldn't want it that way any more but it's still that way for me and I've got a feeling it's always going to be.

So . . . I'll go to that Monday again.

I half thought it all might be a dream, or not a dream exactly, but that you'd have changed your mind over the weekend, or that it had just been one of those funny things that happen, sometimes when two people come together for a moment and the air crackles, then they move away and go cold again.

Like, that movie I was talking about before. At the end they say something like, 'Well, we're all going to be really good friends now,' and one of them says, 'No, we're not, it's just a fluke that this happened, and on Monday we won't want to know each other, we'll be embarrassed to be seen together, we'll pretend this never happened.' And as soon as he says it, or she, I can't remember, you think, Yeah, that's exactly right.

So I really thought there was a big chance it'd be that way for us.

Monday when I saw you coming along the walkway I was shaking like a leaf. And me mates, they didn't know nothing, of course; they thought we was still worst enemies, and Artie was saying, 'Hey Tony, here's your girlfriend,' real sarcastic, and I'll never forget the look on his face when you took my hands and kissed me right on the mouth.

Mmm, your warm firm lips, and your little tongue flicking into mine like a lizard, I forgot about Artie pretty quickly.

Oh fuck it, that's enough for this letter. Bye bye bye bye bye, Miff.

Lots of love,

Tony

Dearest Miff,

There's hardly been any time to write to you the last few days. Sorry about that. Sometimes I wonder if they do it deliberately, make me work my bum off just so I can't sit in the corner of the TV room thinking of you. Do you reckon they'd do that?

Too fucking right they would.

I want to live in a dream world with you, Miff, that's all. I want us to be on a boat, one of those big white bastards, drifting through the beautiful calm blue seas, not going anywhere in particular, just watching all them tropical coloured fish. And we wouldn't wear no clothes, we'd lie around on the deck and make love whenever we felt like it. Your beautiful brown body walking naked towards me. Oh God, Miff, I'm going to do myself damage here just imagining it. Better change the subject, change it real quick. A couple of times thinking about you early on, when we first started going together, I came without even touching myself, never done that before or since. It was out of sight, man. Unreal. That's how much I loved you.

Sometimes you can't hardly believe what your body will do.

OK, change the subject. What to? I don't know, I was just thinking about school and how different it was once we started being together. I lived for the sight of you, Miff. I'd come to school in the morning, get off the scummy old bus with its ripped seats and shitty smelly old Wally the driver, and I'd walk through the staff carpark where we weren't meant to go, round the Lasers and Hyundais and Nissans, all those shitty little clean shiny cars that teachers buy . . . past them and past the main entrance with the sign saying students can't use it—in case we contaminate it or something—along the

covered walkway and the lockers with
doors hanging off and graffiti all over them,
past the rubbish tins that the cleaners never
empty, through the plastic bags blowing
across the bitumen, past the sexual
harassment poster that says if you look at a
girl's legs you're a pervert, past the try-hard
library and the noticeboards with last year's
netball results going yellow and faded, and
there you'd be, Miff, in your tight black
jeans and that plain grey T-shirt, playing
with your long black hair, looking so clean
like you'd just stepped out of the ocean, like
a model in a magazine, just *shining*, shining
like the sun was for you alone, shining like
you were the sun, shining like this special
light came from inside you, a fucking
miracle, and you were a miracle, Miff, you
were the greatest fucking miracle in my life.

After I started going with you I never
wagged school no more, Miff—not unless
you were wagging it with me. I mean, shit,
I didn't do any more work than I had
before, even though you kept giving me a
hard time about it, trying to make me do a
bit, but hey, at least I turned up. Be grateful
for small mercies, OK?

I loved just talking to you, Miff, even
though I never said anything much about
myself. I know you didn't like that, you
kept hassling me about it, asking all them

questions, wanting to know every fucking thing about me. Now I wish I had said more. I'm trying to make up for it by writing these letters, but it's not the same, and anyway it's a bit late. Talking: that's what I should have done more of. It's just that I'm such a dickhead that I couldn't figure it out before. Christ, we fuck ourselves up, don't we Miff? Don't we just fuck ourselves up?

Trouble is, I've never been a talker. You gotta learn how to talk, I reckon. I don't mean just jabber on about footy and shit; I mean talk the way *you* did, about yourself and stuff that happens and whether you should do this or that or something else. I found that pretty fucking hard, still do. I know you did too, don't get me wrong, but you did it better than I ever could.

You know those movies where something bad, something real bad, is about to happen, and the sky gets darker and darker and this music starts, and it's always the same kind of music, real threatening, real scary, it's not exactly music even, just these sounds that are ugly and they don't go together all smooth and nice and sweet like some music do? It's like you can feel the wings of the dark angel beating over your head and you know something terrible's coming and there's nothing, not one fucking

thing, you can do to stop it? That's what it
was like with us Miff; I heard that music, I
heard it getting louder and louder, and there
wasn't nothing anyone could do about it.
It scared the shit out of me but there wasn't
nothing I could do about it.

Ah, fuck it, I don't want to think any
more about that stuff, and besides my
back's hurting like shit tonight, if you really
want to know. I'm gonna go get some of the
magic pills, Miff.

Bye,

Tony

Dear Miff,

They keep coming at me with all this
denial shit, Miff; I mean, what the fuck
would they know? I don't deny nothing, I
know everything that's happened to me and
I know it was my own fucking fault and I
know what it means. I just don't need them
to remind me of it every fucking day and
night. Maybe they want me to be fucking
grateful I'm in this fucking place, but I tell
you what, I got news for them: gratitude
ain't in my fucking vocabulary, not me
baby, so fuck you all.

So what if I just want to dream about the past? So fucking what? It's none of their fucking business.

They reckoned that my uncle and aunt were going to visit yesterday but they never turned up, not that I want them to, anyway.

So you know what I'm going to do, Miff? I'm going to live in the past just a little bit longer—in fact, for as long as I want.

And you're the past I want to live in, Miff.

That's not so bad, is it—to live in the past? Not when the past was like we had. So many good times, so many laughs. Geez, it's a long time since I had a laugh. But that first Monday that we were together: that was the best day of my life, I reckon. The way everyone looked at us! Like they couldn't believe it. They couldn't either. Even with the teachers, man; they were spinning out, like, 'This can't be for real! Tell me it isn't true!'

Cos, of course, everyone knew how much we hated each other's guts before that.

You know what that hate time was like, Miff? It was a zone we had to pass through. And once we'd passed through it we were in a new area, one I hadn't visited before. It was full-on, one-on-one, after that.

Amazing. The world stopped existing outside us two. My uncle and aunt, my father, even my mum if she'd been there, they could be wherever they wanted, they could do whatever they wanted, they could have said any shit to me and I wouldn't have noticed. You and I, we lived on an island that floated through the school, down the streets, through the shopping centre, an island like a little spaceship, and no-one else could get on it.

No-one else had the passport or the visa or the tickets.

First time I went to your place with you was, what? After we'd had about two weeks together? Second time was about ten days later. I didn't really want to go again. You'd been hassling me trying to get an invite to my uncle and aunt's. But I didn't want that, either. I didn't want us to be together at my place or yours. Just in the streets with you, that was enough for me, in the parks, in the wild places.

But because I wanted to do everything right with you I gave in when you said to come the second time. 'No-one'll be there,' you said. Well, I'm not going to give you a hard time about that again. Just because half your fucking family was there. At least your father was away, saving lives or feeling up little girls, or both. I don't know what I would have done if he'd crashed the place.

So, off we went, me talking more and more the closer we got because that's what I do when I'm nervous, that's the only time I talk, but just talking shit, and you talking less and less, because that's what you do. It was pretty weird when I saw the cars there, shit. There was your mother's Alfa and your brother's BM and your sister's Jeep. Like, that was a quiet day for you guys. Awesome. I don't know why I didn't piss off straightaway. Should have. I knew when I saw the cars that there were people home, and you knew it too, of course. I felt you getting more nervous—but you told me it'd be cool, so in we went.

It wasn't too cool, though. For one thing, I couldn't believe the way you talked to each other, Miff! I mean, I know these were your family and I don't want to put shit on them, but you were all so fucking polite, it really got to me! It was like a conversation on TV or at the doctor's; you know, when that lady—I forget what they call them—she sits behind the desk and takes all your particulars, she talks like, 'Good morning, Mrs Marchesi. I'm sorry, Doctor's running a little late today. How long since you were last here? How would you like to pay for this?'

That's what it was like! I couldn't believe that. It was the last thing I expected.

We came into that big room where you've got the big TV and all them lounges and magazines and shit, and the mirrors that you nearly walk right through because you think it's the other half of the room, and there was your mother and your sister and your brother. I was bloody red as a beetroot, didn't know which way to look, and they're acting cool as if you bring home some loser like me every day, and your mother says, 'Oh, there you are, darling. We were starting to wonder what happened to you,' when I know and you know and everyone else down the east coast must know that you did what you bloody liked and no-one in your family would have a clue from one week to the next where you were or what you were doing or who you were with.

'And this must be Tony.' That was her second line. Cracked me right up, only I was too scared to laugh. I shook her hand but it felt like a bit of lettuce that's been out of the fridge a week or so. I couldn't look at her. Too embarrassing. Then I had to meet your brother and sister. They didn't seem too interested.

'Where do you live, Tony?' Already your mother was into the questions. There was no way I was going to give the right answers; I mean the answers she wanted. She wanted you hanging round with private school boys who talked like your brother. The street I was living in then, I don't think she'd heard of it. I don't think she'd even heard of the suburb.

Miff, sometimes—I don't like to say this but I've gotta be honest—sometimes I wondered if you just went with me because I was the opposite of the kind of guy your parents'd want.

Like, you were using me to say 'fuck you' to your parents. Not, like, deliberately—but sometimes I did wonder if that was what was going down.

Anyway, I'm not getting into that, I was just trying to remember how it all went that day. Seems to me it was nothing but a whole lot of questions. All hidden under your mother's super-cool super-polite voice. 'What are your favourite subjects?' 'And what do you want to do when you leave school, Tony?' 'Is that what your father does?' 'You don't think that some kind of tertiary course would be a good idea?'

And so on. By the time we escaped and you took me upstairs I was bloody shaking. We got into your room and I couldn't relax at all. You grabbed me and kissed me but I couldn't get into it. I said to you, 'Is that the way they always talk?' And you didn't even know what I was on about!

'What do you mean?' you asked.

What did I fucking mean? I thought it'd be obvious to anyone who wasn't a sandwich short of a lunchbox.

'The way they fucking talk to you, like you're a fucking stranger, is that what it's always like? They're so fucking polite! Don't you guys ever, you know, *talk*?'

'Well, what's it like at your place?'

You sounded so puzzled. I couldn't believe it.

'Well fuck it, my uncle and aunt, we don't talk either, but we're not bloody polite. If someone gives you the shits you just scream at them! My uncle doesn't bloody sit around saying, "Oh dear, do you think Tony's playing that music a little bit loud?" He sticks his head out of the TV room and he yells, "Turn the fucking music down before I come down there and put a fucking baseball bat through your fucking CD!" If they're pissed off because they don't know where I've been they're yelling at me, like: "Where the fuck have you been?" not "Oh, we were starting to wonder what had happened to you."'

Of course, I forgot that in your house everyone's rooms are about a hundred metres away from each other so you wouldn't hear their CDs. And anyway, they'd be playing opera or something. And, even if it was too loud, you'd just say, 'Oh, excuse me, Miffany, we were wondering if you would mind making a tiny little adjustment to your volume switch.'

I don't know which is better, but; I mean my uncle and aunt gave me the shits with all the arguments, and so did my mum and dad before that, but at least you knew what everyone thought. With your family you wouldn't have a clue what they thought about anything. The only message that came through loud and clear was that I wasn't the kind of guy they would have signed up for their daughter to go with. But I figured that was their problem. It only made me more determined. That's the way I am, Miff, you know that. I'm a stubborn son-of-a-bitch. And I don't give up easy.

Trouble is, what I just wrote, I don't know if it's true any more. Since I fucked up so bad. I wish you were here to tell me, Miff. I can't work these things out for myself now. Am I tough, am I weak, am I pathetic? I don't know. And maybe it's the not knowing that's the worst thing of all.

T o n y

Dear Miff,

Geez, I've had it up to here, Miff. All the things they say to me, it's like they hate my guts, like they want to attack me. Insults, all the time insults. I mean, who the fuck do they think they are? Cindy, she's a girl here, she reckons they're doing it deliberately because they reckon I'm too passive or something. That 'denial' stuff I was talking to you about one time.

Today this dickhead called Tom who works here told me how he reckons when I get the shits I lash out at the nearest target, doesn't matter who it is. He reckons it's really me I'm angry at. What a lot of bullshit. I don't know why I listened to him. Normally I never listen to these bastards. I write letters to you instead. I'd rather do that any day.

It's all because I cracked at this little kid this morning. Little shit. I was in the gym and thought I'd have a go for once, so I had this neck thing and I was pulling against it and I would have got it going, Miff, I swear I would, no worries, but this kid distracted me, started laughing, and I was so pissed off I slagged at him, like spat right in his face. Didn't mean nothing by it, just wanted to shut him up, make him think before he gets so fucking sarcastic next time. So now everyone here hates me. What do you reckon, new experience for me, hey?

I don't give a flying fuck; they hated me before this, anyway.

Actually what this Tom bloke really said was that I lash out at someone weaker. That's not a very nice thing to say, is it, Miff?

You know it's not true, don't you, Miff?

There was that time at school, though. You were pissed off at me that day. See, the thing was my dad had been visiting my uncle and aunt the night before and they'd been drinking all day and my dad was trying to pick me and I was just in a bad mood. I know I did the wrong thing, but. Some of those Year 7s but, they're too fucking cheeky for their own good. Some of them really ask for it. I wouldn't do it again though, Miff. You gotta believe that.

Anyway you were no angel yourself, Miff. Geez, you cracked me up with some of the shit you did. The big difference was you got away with it most of the time and I never did. They was always watching out for me. Like those keys of Mrs McVeigh's, I'd never have got away with them. Well, she'd never have given them to me in the first place. You had it so well worked out, but. She never suspected a thing. 'Oh Mrs McVeigh, Mr Stadley said can he have a key for the costume cupboard please?'

You'd worked out she'd have to give you a master key because you'd heard Stadley say that he had the only key in the school for the costume cupboard. Then you have me on me bike waiting and on your way back from the hall you give me the key and I'm down to the hardware and back in fifteen minutes, then you're into Mrs McVeigh's cool as you like, cos I'm the one who's worked up the sweat. Then you take Stadley's keys back to him. 'Oh, look Mr Stadley, I found them. Guess where they were?'

In your fucking pocket the whole time, that's where they were.

I reckon you'd be good at organising a bank job or something, Miff.

You could pull off anything. And I mean anything. I ought to know. That's a joke by the way, Miff, just thought I'd better say.

But hey, Miff, didn't we have a time with that master key? For two months we had ourselves a party with it. Be having one now if you hadn't lost the fucker. I still reckon Murphy pinched it. Only thing we didn't think to do was make another copy for ourselves. We were a bit dumb about that. I'm still spewing about it. We could have got Mrs McVeigh's again, but somehow we never got around to it.

'Geez, we got into everything though, didn't we? The canteen, that was the best one. We were both so fucking stoned. We had the munchies bad. Had to get them corn chips, didn't we, Miff? Just had to have them corn chips. That big brown door with our names scratched into it. I cracked up when I saw them, in their little heart. I'd forgotten we'd done that. Between me cracking up and you getting the giggles and the door squeaking and grinding as it opened I don't know how we didn't get busted. But next thing we're in there with the door shut behind us. It was fucking dark and fucking scary but, geez, talk about a kid in a candy shop. We had ourselves an all right time. Those fucking Freddos, I must have eaten ten of the bastards. I've never been able to look at a Freddo again. But you pigged out on the Caramello Bears, remember that? God, it was a pisser. I fair dinkum thought I was going to chuck before I got out of there. And then I was shitting myself getting out because I didn't know if Hammond or Fishbum or the security guy or even Paspaley might have been waiting for us.

You're sort of dropping into nothing coming out of a place like that, just hoping like hell they won't be standing in a line with their arms folded, a fucking reception committee. It was like bungy jumping would be, I reckon.

After that we went up on the hill and you wanted to have sex and I was rolling around the grass holding my guts in, going, 'Oh God, why'd I eat all that shit?' Sex was the last thing I felt like.

That was the opposite of the way it was most of the time, hey?

The other good gag with the key was getting in the Admin office, especially Paspaley's office, and checking out all the school secrets. And the staffroom. I pigged out again, on Tim Tams this time. But the school secrets were pretty boring. We read our files—most of it just garbage about being on probation and dropping Indonesian and getting busted for wagging. There was that stuff from the psychologist, but—about how I'm a genius and fucking it up by being unmotivated or whatever they call it. I just laughed when I showed it to you but to tell you the truth, Miff, I felt a bit of a buzz when I read it. I mean, geez, I've always thought I was the big dummy, and when teachers went on about how 'if you only settled down and did some serious work' I thought it was the same bullshit line they give every student.

Not that it made any difference, but fuck it, I'd rather be brainy than dumb.

Your file was really thin but there was one thing I hadn't known, that stuff about you hacking up your wrist last year. I was really shocked, Miff. Most of all I was shocked that you hadn't told me. I guess you giving me the file to read was your way of telling me. I know you were watching me when I did read it. I admit I blinked a few times. I'd always thought you were strong; maybe that was the first time I realised you weren't strong inside; it was all a bluff, an act.

Like I say, it was a shock. I looked at you differently after that.

Next time we made love I picked up your wrist and checked it out. Do you remember? I bet you do. That faint white line, I'd never noticed it before. It scared the shit out of me, that white line. I kissed it so you wouldn't see my lips trembling. I heard the loud ugly music that night for sure, Miff. I felt the dark angel right there above us.

He never went away though, did he, Miff? He was always there hovering over our heads. As long as we were together he

was going to be there. He was just waiting
for us cos he knew he was going to get us in
the end, that bastard.

See you,

Tony

Dear Miff,

This is the first time I've written to
you in the morning, Miff. It's about six
o'clock and already there's a bit of
movement at this station. Sure is a
happening place. I couldn't sleep again last
night, can't sleep now, won't sleep tonight,
won't ever sleep again.

You know something, Miff, there was
this family in Italy I think they were, and
the whole family had insomnia, like none of
them could sleep, and they passed it on
from generation to generation, and Miff,
you won't believe this, some of them died
from it. Can you imagine that? Dying from
not sleeping? Mate, that would be the worst
thing. But all I can think of as I lie here
awake is that family, and how you can die
from that. Geez, it drives me crazy. I just get
this feeling that I'm going to die as I'm
bloody lying on this hard old bed. Weird,

hey? Better not tell them here or you know
where they'll send me.

I think what made me want to write to
you is just that I'm missing you so much.
It's bad this morning. Tell you the truth,
Miff, I'm randy as hell, and writing this
isn't helping any. God, I'd love to lie against
you now and feel your warm naked skin,
feel your firm-soft tits, put myself into you,
feel your wetness, the most exciting feeling
in the world, that wetness, Miff. Christ,
how I loved that wetness. There'll never be
a feeling to equal that in my life.

A lot of things about sex with you were
good, Miff, but you know what I liked
most? Don't laugh, but it was lying together
afterwards stroking each other's back. Just
that, that's all. God, I could have stayed
there all day every day doing nothing else.
I'd give anything to do that now, anything
except my balls. Ha ha. (Joke.)

I'd had a bit of sex before I met you,
Miff. Well, face it, we both had, but with
the others it was just a quick poke. You
were the first one I really, you know, took
the trouble with; wanted to—I feel dumb
saying this—wanted to, you know, please.
Yeah, that was the difference. Is that what
people mean when they talk about love?
Fucked if I know.

My first time, you kept asking, trying

71

to find out, but I wouldn't tell you. First time was when I was a little tacker, with a girl in Year 8. She was a bit of a goer, Stacey, you never met her, she lives in bloody New Zealand now, and she dragged me off to her bed one night at her birthday party when everyone else was watching a video (but they knew what we was doing) and she took my virginity. I still couldn't even shoot. But I liked it. I was nervous but. Next time was with Stacey again about six months later, bit different that time. I could come all right by then, and I sure got into it. We were at the beach and she was with this bloke who was about twenty-six or something fucking stupid, and he had this panel van and he was so pissed he went to sleep right on the beach—burnt so bad you could smell the fucking pork sizzling—and I thought this is my chance, and I got Stacey in the back of the van and had her bikini bottom down around her ankles before she knew what hit her. She was pretty pissed herself as a matter of fact. You're not too good on the grog at that age. I wasn't pissed, but. I'd stayed cold bloody sober cos I'd thought I might have a chance if I kept my eyes open.

Doing it with Stace wasn't much different to wanking, but, if you really want to know. Christ, she was a slut. Fourteen years old and a total write-off.

Then I had the hots for this chick in Year 10. I was in Year 8 still, would you believe. Bit of a laugh. But I thought she was the bloody pin-up of the century. She knew how I felt, too, but she just thought it was a big joke. It wasn't to me. I was deadly serious. Then one night at this party she was really pissed and we done it out the back on the grass. Wasn't that good, but. And afterwards she pretended she was too pissed to even remember, but she did, and I knew she did and she knew I knew she did, etc. etc. But she wouldn't have anything to do with me after that.

The others didn't amount to much. I had the hots for Emma for a while but she wouldn't let me touch her. I rooted Kylie to do her a favour, she was after me for months. Christ, she was ugly, but. Then we pulled a train on Sharon one night when we were off our faces. It took me about five minutes just to get it up.

I did it with Becky a few times. She was OK.

It was so different with you, Miff. You just wouldn't believe how different. I don't know why, except that you were so fucking beautiful, plus you were the only girl I ever met who could match it with me. By the time I figured out you weren't that tough it didn't seem to matter any more.

For a while I thought I'd met my match.

You wanted to have sex that afternoon at your house but I didn't. It was all too weird, me being there, and your mother and all them being downstairs. I couldn't get in the mood at all. I'd wanted to have it with you so badly and there you were handing it to me on a plate and I was knocking it back. Crazy. But it just didn't feel right.

When we did have it, it took me by surprise. I didn't think we'd have a chance that particular day. Normally on those fucking excursions they guard you like you're on day release from the slammer. Not far wrong, hey? School is like prison, if you ask me. But Mr Rossi, he's not a bad bloke, and all Art teachers are slack. It was a fucking slack excursion, I know that. That fucking gallery's so fucking boring. The only painting I liked was that big nude bitch on the end wall in the big hall and you wouldn't let me perv on her for long. Maybe it did get you a little bit excited though. Maybe you wanted to compete with her? Maybe you thought, 'Huh, I've got more than that slut any day.' Huh Miff, what do you reckon? Am I on to it?

Anyway, whatever. I know it got me a bit fired up, that painting, and I started to hang out for some action. I was giving your ear an erotic experience and you were giggling and pushing me away. The only thing that stopped me going further was all the people around, and Mr Rossi. Like, he might be a good bloke, but if he finds two of his students having sex in the middle of an excursion he's not exactly going to give us a pat on the head and an *A* in Art.

So there we were, both wanting it, all fired up and nowhere to go, surrounded by sex but couldn't hardly touch each other. Till we got into that little room. It was all my idea and I'm proud of it. We went right past the door and then I dragged you back and said, 'Let's check this out,' and you said, 'Oh yeah, art by disabled lesbians, good one,' but I knew what I was after. We were in there about twenty minutes fartarsing around and in all that time no-one else came near the place, and finally I said to you, 'I don't think too many people are interested in art by disabled lesbians,' and right away you knew it was serious and what I was getting at and then I grabbed you and away we went. I'd never done it with so many clothes on before; it was pretty funny when I think about it now, but we weren't laughing at the time.

Geez, we were lucky no-one came in, but. I can't believe we were that dumb.

Oh, but God, I loved it, Miff. I get a lump in my throat thinking about it now. And a lump in my pants, sure, but the look of you afterwards, as you pulled up your undies and gave me this kind of half-smiling half-serious look with your beautiful clear eyes, like you were saying, 'Well, we've done it now. This is getting serious. We're in this for the long haul,' I loved you so much I wanted to pull you down on the floor and take all your clothes off and do it long and slow and forever.

Sex! It rules! Wish we could do it all day every day. Wouldn't get much else done, but.

Second time was at Donald's, the next Friday, when he had that party. That was good timing. We got there early, said hello to a few people, walked through the lounge room and the kitchen, went straight upstairs to his bedroom, locked the door and made love all night. A few people were pissed off with us that night! Especially Donald. I thought he was going to break his own door down at about three o'clock. Just shows, it pays to get to parties early.

Didn't help Donald, but. He got there before anyone else and ended up with nothing.

I didn't need grog or dope or no shit at all that night, Miff. You were the greatest drug ever invented. You were all I ever wanted. When I was with you the sun and moon and stars were in the fucking room, and heaven was in your mouth and your breasts and between your legs. Hell was a long long way away when you were there, Miff. The sun rose and set every time you breathed, and those dark wings and that bad music got pushed off into nowhere.

Funny, you know, I'm writing this surrounded by fucking chaos. Fucking chaos and darkness. The nurses have been in and out about sixteen times saying it's time to get up. They want to get me up and I've just been refusing the whole time. It's past eight o'clock. This is getting heavy, to tell you the truth. I might stop writing, I think, but I'm fucked if I'll get up. Why should I. What's to get up to? I feel like staying in bed all day so I'll stay in bed all day. Fuck the lot of them.

Bye, bye Miff,

T o n y

D e a r   M i f f ,

Geez, am I ever in the doghouse here. They've all got the shits with me now—even Tracy, who's the nicest one of the lot. She's not a full nurse, she's a SEN, but I like her the best. She was in here a minute ago giving me the big lecture. 'Your attitude's so negative, Tony. Everyone wants to help you but you're not giving them a chance.'

Well, what I reckon is, what's to be positive above? Why shouldn't I be fucking negative? Who wouldn't be? I didn't want this. Just because I fucked up, now I'm being punished. What I can't get my head around is how long it's for. And even Tracy doesn't have the least idea, not the least faint glimmering of the slightest tiny idea, what it's like, how it feels, what I think about it all.

'Denial' they reckon. Too fucking right I'm in denial, and I'm planning to stay that way, believe me.

And in the meantime I'm getting treated like shit. All these privileges withdrawn. Privileges, that's a joke. Being allowed to breathe around here, that's a privilege.

So now I'm not allowed to watch TV or play the computers or get stuff from the canteen. I just get people to buy stuff for me, but, so that's no problem. And there's not many other privileges they can take off me. Like phone calls. I don't get any, do I, so that's easy.

Well, up their bums, I say. I don't have to do what they say. I never did what anyone said before I come in here so I don't see why I should start now.

Wonder where you are, Miff, and what you're doing tonight. Wonder if you're thinking about me. I still can't believe what happened, the way it worked out. I guess that's what they mean by denial. It's a bit of a mess, isn't it? I never thought it'd go this way. Lucky we can't see the future, hey? Guess it'd have been better if we never got involved with each other in the first place. I don't like thinking about that, but.

Maybe when you're as much in love as we were it can't never last, Miff. Maybe the only ones that last are the ones that aren't that serious, you know, the ones that are just mucking around. The ones that are only out for a good time, like I was before I met you. Maybe when you're our age you aren't meant to get serious.

We thought what we had was so strong we could beat everyone. Your parents, my uncle and aunt, the teachers, everyone. We thought we could take on the world.

I wish you'd never kept getting me to come to your place, but. It might have been different if I hadn't started going there so regular. I don't know why I did go. It was easy, I guess, and better than my uncle and aunt's. And I was sort of fascinated by how rich you were. For a long time I never felt comfortable there, but it got easier, until I got to really like being in your room. Never liked the rest of the house, but. Although if none of your family was there it wasn't too bad.

When they were home they treated me like such a piece of shit. I don't think you realised how bad it was, cos you didn't want to know about it, and they kind of did it behind your back. After a while I sussed that you hated me talking about it, so I used to shut up. But it cut me deep, Miff, you better believe it, when your brother looked at me with his weak soft eyes like a fucking guinea pig and said shit like, 'Don't you have a home of your own to go to?' like it was a joke, cos I was there so much for a while, only it wasn't no fucking joke.

And your sister, one day she said to me, 'Why do you say "youse" all the time, Tony? Don't you know how terrible it sounds and how people judge you by it?'

And all I could think of to say was, 'Well, Miff doesn't judge me by it,' and she just rolled her eyes like, 'Miffy, don't talk to me about Miffy.'

Fucking bitch. They were all the same. Your mother. Did you notice the way she never looked at me when she was talking to me? Her eyes were always off-centre, looking over my shoulder. Like I was some bit of dog shit that she'd stepped in when some fucking mongrel had an accident on the carpet.

Not that any dog would dare lay a shit in your house.

Those rich houses, the worst thing that goes wrong in them is when the fucking clock is a minute slow. Then it's like, 'Oh my God, throw it away, get another one.' It's like the leaves know not to fall on your tennis court, the grass knows not to grow above a certain height. No-one pisses in your pool. Houses like yours, they're like churches. No-one acts real bad, no-one goes wild in them.

That's why I never made love to you too often there. Not that I couldn't get it up or anything dumb like that: just that I didn't feel like it. Not until that day. For the first time I felt OK there that day. The sun was shining, the birds were singing . . . No, serious, do you remember? We'd had all that rain? Geez, it rained for a month, it felt like. My bedroom was leaking in about sixteen places: it had fucking mildew up the walls. And this is the house you were so red-hot keen to visit. I had buckets and saucepans and shit all over the place, then my aunt'd want to cook something so she'd

come in and take a couple of the saucepans.
And the next thing I'd be up to me ankles
in water.

But at last the rain stopped and it was
all beautiful and stuff, and I felt so good, so
high, like I was a kite with the sky opening
up, parting in front of me, and I was going
into it till I was out of sight. Unreal. It's
weird how the weather does that to you,
changes your mood.

So I didn't feel all sick and nervous
going to your place, like I normally would.
I just about danced down the bloody street.

It's strange, because you know how I
said before about the movies where the sky
gets darker and the dark angel's beating his
wings and it means something bad's
coming? Wouldn't you think I would have
felt those wings, Miff? Wouldn't you think
we both would have felt them wings? But I
didn't. I don't know if you did; maybe: you
did seem a bit strange, and you didn't say
too much, but I never asked you about that.
Didn't get a chance.

And it was so good when we found that
no-one was home. It seemed like everything
was going perfect, nothing could possibly
go wrong. We went upstairs. I couldn't
wait. I was all over you and you were all
over me. Clothes were flying like they was
autumn leaves and there was a willy-willy

in the room. Then we was rolling on the bed, going for it, full on. I couldn't stop myself, I come all over you in about a minute and a half, sorry about that, but I did better the second time, hey? And the third. Am I showing off now? Sorry. Again.

Then there was that nice part that I said about before: just you and me lying there, nothing on, your hands down my back, so warm, touching and stroking and petting me, and me doing the same to you. Pretty good, hey? I could have stayed like that forever.

We must have been lying there, I don't know how long, could have been a week, I was that spaced out. The room was warm: like, being upstairs it got warmer than downstairs, and being a hot day, it was so good in there. Then it all changed. So sudden. We never heard nothing, never had no warning, nothing. One minute perfect, the next minute totally and utterly fucked. Well, they say you never see the one that gets you. First thing I knew was this cold blast on my bum, and your hand against me got so cold all of a sudden. It stopped stroking me and stuck there like a little block of ice. I knew something was wrong, something was terribly wrong, and I didn't dare turn or look around. I guess I was a bit frozen myself. Then your mother let rip

with this hell of a scream. I jumped up,
I didn't know what to do or where to go, I
was just running around in circles grabbing
for me clothes and trying to find stuff and
shaking like crazy. I didn't mean to hit her,
Miff, it was just the way she was screaming,
I couldn't stand it, then what she said, she
shouldn't have said that, about me being
filth and all, she didn't have the right to say
that. I mean it's not like any of it was my
fault, you were just as much to blame.
Christ, I can't believe how much everything
changed in one moment. She was lying on
the floor with blood coming out of her nose
and you were standing there in the nude
with your hands up to your face staring at
her. You didn't seem to see me at all. It was
like I didn't exist any more for you. I tried
to tell you it was an accident, that I didn't
mean it, and then I tried to help your mum,
and I was starting to realise it was, like,
serious, she was hurt pretty bad, but then
you started screaming at me too, like I was
a monster or something, and I couldn't
stand it, I just had to get out of there. It
sounded like your mother's voice all over
again. I was running down the stairs with
only half me clothes on, them screams
following me all the way down the stairs,
all the way down the street, everywhere I
went. Didn't matter how fast I ran or how

far, them screams just wouldn't get out of me ears. I can still hear them now, you know, Miff, still hear them fucking screams.

T.

Dear Miff,

The weirdest thing ever happened today. I had a visitor. And you want to know who? You'll never guess in a million and one years. Fucking Hammond! Fucking Hammond! See, told you you'd never guess. I couldn't believe it when he walked in. What's he want with me? Buggered if I know. When they told me I had a visitor I was hoping it might be me dad, to tell you the truth. Some hope. It was pretty bloody weird when I realised who it was. Not much of a conversation but I don't know what he expected. I'm not too interested in footy or cricket or school, especially now that I can't do none of that stuff. He raved on for about ten minutes about how the footy team was runners-up and stuff, but then he sort of realised I didn't give a shit.

Anyway, at least he went to the trouble. It's a fair way out, this place, but I guess he'd have a car, him being a teacher and all.

I didn't ask how he got here. I didn't talk too much. Couldn't think of nothing to say. He soon ran out of stuff, too. Not much anyone can say about what's happened. This place gets people a bit, when they first see it—I know it freaked me out when they brought me in. All these fucking specimens, like a fucking zoo. Some of them are all right when you get to know them, but. Some of them aren't.

So anyway, there we were, sitting around like old buddies, chewing the fat. Bit different to being in his office, hey? First time I've talked to him that I wasn't in trouble. Hey, did you know he's got kids? Poor little buggers, imagine being his kids. I don't know, he's probably not that bad as a dad, he'd be good for helping with your homework, anyway. He told me about all these kids at school, like Nick, reckons he's got a job at Food Plus, doing all right. Georgie's moved to Queensland, he reckons. Sal, Salvatore, I forgot to ask about him. Dino, he didn't know much about him, still at school, nothing much different there. That'd be Dino, nothing'll ever change with him, I reckon.

Course the one person we didn't talk about was you. That was half the trouble: there was that many things we couldn't talk about, there was fuck all left to say.

I was glad when he got up to go. I don't want no-one feeling sorry for me, I don't want no charity. Most times I just reckon I'll wait till I get out of here then I'll go catch that fucking train and do it properly. I won't fuck up again.

So anyway, he went and I don't think he'll be back for a while. I didn't exactly give him that good a time. I reckon he'll find better ways to spend his weekends from now on. I wonder what he does do in his spare time? Probably reads Maths books, or tortures budgies or something.

No, I shouldn't bag him, at least he took the fucking trouble to come here. No-one else has bothered.

Wonder if he will come back? Be a hundred to one, I reckon. He's probably driving home right now thinking, What a waste of fucking time that was. I could have stayed home and watched TV. Except he wouldn't swear, being a teacher.

No, just kidding, I know teachers swear. But I don't think he would, somehow. He's not the swearing type.

I still can't get over him coming here, but. I mean Hammond, God, no bastard gave me a harder time than he did and there wasn't no bastard I gave a harder time to than him. Tell you what, if he was in a place like this I wouldn't have visited him.

I would have fucking celebrated. Bit sick, hey? But then I always was a sick bugger.

I did make a bit of an effort in gym today though, Miff. You would have been proud of me. Fucking Len just about fell over. Just as long as he doesn't think I'm going to make a habit of it.

See ya,

T o n y

D e a r   M i f f ,

You know what these cunts want now? They want to send me to a fucking psych unit. Good one. Real good one. That's all I need: to be told I'm psycho. They're fucking psycho themselves, if you ask me. Half the fucking staff are weird. I mean who'd want to work in a fucking dump like this, anyway? You'd have to be sick in the head, hanging around all day with fucking retards like us. Fucking bastards, fuck them all, I hate the lot of them, I won't talk to them and they reckon it's because I'm psycho. Well, it's not. It's because they're fucking retards themselves. And now I hate them even more. That's the last time I make any effort, the last time I try in gym or do any fucking thing for them. I mean, geez, Miff, last week fucking Dillon said he'd heard I was improving, and now this. There's no way I'm going there, no fucking way. I don't care what they do, they can't make me, I'll fucking yell the fucking place down. That's the trouble with being this way, you've got no fucking control. But I swear, even if they fucking drag me there I'll make their lives so fucking miserable that they'll have me back here before they've even changed the sheets on my fucking bed. I absolutely totally swear that on the fucking Bible or any other fucking book you want to name, that is the truth, so help me God. I know what it'll be like, all these fucking crazies out of their trees, hanging off the ceiling telling you they're Elvis Presley or something. I'm not psycho, Miff, I swear. I know I'm not. I don't belong in a place like that. I am not not not not not going there. I can't Miff, I'd die in a place like that. I'd just lie right down and die.

Oh God, Miff, I can't believe how I've messed up: how much I've totally fucked up my life. I mean, geez, Miff, look at me, I'm only fucking sixteen and already my life is totally wrecked. How could I have made such a mess of everything, Miff? I didn't mean to. I didn't mean any of this, it just happened, I don't know how. I still don't know how I got it so wrong. I'm sorry about your mum, Miff. I didn't want to hurt her, I never wanted to hurt anyone, I've got this terrible temper, you know that. I was just born with it, I guess. It's got me in so much trouble. I wish I could cut it out and throw it away, like, amputate it. These fucking counsellors here, they go on and on about all the things you can do in the future, and I don't even listen. I don't give a flying fuck. I don't want any of them, I just want things to be back the way they were. I want to be lying with you on your bed again, with your body all hot under me and your tits pressing into me. Like I said before, I'll probably never have sex with anyone again, and without sex I reckon there's no fucking life anyway. And in a psych ward, what's going to happen? Like I know I'm not psycho now, but who knows? After a week in there I'll be dribbling down my chin and having some nurse feeding me with a spoon and me not knowing whether I'm the Pope or Captain Caveman or Flipper the fucking dolphin. And I'm not fucking joking, Miff. I wish I could joke about it but how can you joke about something like this? As if everything else that's happened to me isn't enough, now they have to go and add this to the list. It's too much, Miff, it's just too fucking much. If they were setting out to break me, and that's what I reckon sometimes, then they've just about done it now. They can go home tonight feeling proud, like they've achieved something. 'How was your day, dear?' 'Good thank you, darling. We finally did it today; we finally destroyed that little bastard Tony. It's taken us a long time but we've done it at last. God, it was good, we actually had him crying and begging, it was fair up him I reckon: he's been asking for it long enough. But we sure got him a good one. Ha ha ha. Get us a beer will you, love.'

The whole world's against you, Miff, against everyone, I mean, that's what I've learned. Your life's a solo run, and even the crowd that's cheering want you to fall over. They love you when you win but they love it even better when you lose. I used to think I'd be a winner one day, Miff, but now I know I'm the biggest loser ever. I've set new records for losing. I'm such a loser I'm a winner—the world champion at losing. Joke, hey? Shit, that's two jokes in one letter. Funny how when I'm crying is when I start making jokes. Maybe I am fucking sick. Better quit before I make another joke. Three in one letter might be a bit much

even for you. And if these cunts find out
about them they'll have me in that psych
unit for sure.

Tony

Dear Miff,

I haven't written to you in so long.
No fucking wonder, I've been too fucked
in the head to pick up a pen. This fucking
ward's a crazy place all right, but not as
bad as I thought it would be. Some of the
kids are all right. It's only some of the
adults who are really psycho.

They're all so shit scared of me, though.
I don't know what it is, being in this thing
maybe. Or maybe someone told them about
me. Or maybe it's just me: that's the kind of
person I am, a monster. Little kids scream
and run when they see me. That'd figure.
Why wouldn't they? Anyway, whatever it is,
no-one comes near me. It's strange that: I
can't get used to being a monster, but I go
with it, I'm not going to fight it, if that's
how they want it then fuck them, let them
see me that way.

Turns out I'm not even meant to be here
because it's minimum security; well, it's no

security really, but I guess they think I'm safe. Anyway Hilary, the social worker, reckons it's some great big deal getting me in, like I'm meant to be grateful! Grateful! Oh yeah, I'm fucking grateful. I'll be writing a thank you letter to the Department, no worries. Thank you for putting me in the nuthouse, really good of you, thanks a lot.

There's this girl here, reminds me of you a bit, Miff, talks like you, posh accent and all that. When she does talk, which is about once a week. We've got that in common. She's nice looking but I don't think she's going to be dropping round to see me too often.

Just listening to them all talking about each other, which is like their favourite hobby, their full-time occupation, they reckon her dad was some real rich cunt, real famous, in the papers and all that, only now he's in the slammer, so it's fair up his bum.

That's where your dad should be.

This place is pretty fucking slack you know. It's a lot better than the facility. You don't have to do anything if you don't want, especially me, because they're scared of me. And the food's all right, not bad anyway. Like tonight it was chicken Kiev and cherry pie and you could have any flavour ice-cream you wanted. Hell of a lot better than at my uncle and aunt's, that's for sure. My aunt was the worst fucking cook. She only knew three recipes: pizza, lasagne and spaghetti bolognaise. And she's not even Italian. Geez, I got sick of pizza. Most of the time she didn't cook it anyway, just got takeaway.

They try to teach you all this shit here like conflict resolution, 'alternatives to violence'. I don't know about that stuff. I'm not that interested.

Something this kid here was saying though, this crazy girl called Jacqui, made me think. Just about the way my life was, way back. When my parents was together. I'd forgotten a lot of that shit. I don't think I really wanted to remember it, to tell you the truth. Man, they was bad times. All this fighting and screaming and shit, and then my little brother dying, poor little bugger. At least he got out of life the easy way. I wonder what he'd think now if he saw me like this. Guess he wouldn't think I was much of a brother, would he? Little brothers are meant to look up to their older brothers, aren't they? Hope he doesn't know what happened, wherever he is.

You hear these kids talk, it's like they're from another planet. Most of them are real posh, go to private schools, stuff like that.

I don't think they've got much in common with me. They think they've got problems, fucking hell, they must be joking. They don't know when they're well off.

To them a big problem is having a zit, like they need six months' counselling if they have a fucking zit, that's how sad their lives are.

Oh, not all of them, I guess. Some of them are pretty fucked up.

To hear the way they go on, though, you'd think there's a competition to be the most fucked in the head. Like they're always trying to prove that they're more fucked up than the next person. Can you believe it? I'm the most fucked-up one here and I'm not happy about it, I don't want to win any medals.

I'm not happy, Miff, and that's the truth. But the truth is that I'm not going to be happy anywhere. That's a real problem.

T.

Dear Miff,

Geez, the months have rolled on, haven't they? I must have been having a hell of a lot of fun, because the time has flown like a Calibra turbo. Didn't have nothing to do tonight, so thought I'd bring you up to date on my life.

I don't know where to start, but. It's pretty boring for me, writing down stuff I already know. One day I ought to send all these fucking letters, God knows where. God knows where you are, where you're living. Maybe you're not even living. Maybe you're dead. I never thought about that before. I just scared the shit out of myself thinking about it then. I don't want you to be dead, Miff, I want you to be safe, to be OK, to have forgotten all about me and how I wrecked your life. I know you and your mum had fights all the time and you used to say you hated her, but I don't think you hated her too much. It's just the way a lot of kids talk, you know what I mean? It don't mean a lot sometimes. Sure it was different for me, with my mum pissing off and all, but your mum was OK, just trying to do the right thing by you, even if she was a snob and all that.

I been thinking about my mum a bit lately. You know, wondering where she is. Thinking I might even try to find her. Don't know why. Don't owe her nothing. She sure cleaned us out when she left. Geez, I'll never forget that day till I'm dead and rotting. I never thought she'd leave. I mean they had fights and stuff but everyone's parents are like that, they always fight, don't they? And I thought things had been getting better, shows what a great bloody judge I am. They hadn't had a real full-on fight for a few weeks but I guess she was just getting ready for the midnight flit. Midday flit in her case. Don't know how she could have done it, but—not because of me or me dad, Christ, anyone would want to piss off on us, we were no bloody prizes, that's for sure—but me little brother, Owen, he was only a year old. I don't know how she could have pissed off on him, I reckon that was a bit rough. But the thing that was a real shocker, this is really rank, she took all his toys. Every bloody one. I mean, I come home from school and she'd cleaned the place out. I walked into his room, it was always the first thing I did when I got home from school, and I just couldn't believe it, it were totally bare, just Owen lying in his cot crying, like he knew something was wrong. Bloody lucky he still had his cot if you ask me.

I stood there like an idiot, looking around, trying to work out what was going on. I thought we'd been burgled. I still didn't wake up to what had happened till Dad got home, a few minutes after. He took one look and he knew. He went berserk.

She'd taken everything: the cooking things, the video, the lightglobes, the dunny paper. Can you believe it? The dunny paper. Even this little bunny I'd bought Owen for his first birthday, she took that. Plus all his clothes. Dad reckoned she was probably pregnant to some other bloke and she wanted the stuff for the new kid. But she had no right to take the rabbit, I mean it wasn't hers. It really gives me the shits to think of some other kid playing with Owen's bunny.

No wonder the poor little bugger died: no mum and no bunny and no rattle and no rubber cat that squeaked when you pressed its tail. No wonder he didn't feel like hanging around. I mean that day she took off, she just left him there in his little cot, not giving a shit whether he'd be all right or not. Lucky me and me dad weren't late home for once.

So I don't know why I'd want to spend three seconds of my time thinking about me mum or wanting to find her. But something in me just won't let go of the idea. I been thinking about her night and day, to tell you the truth. More than the bit that I said at the start of the letter. I sort of think she'll be able to fix everything up for me somehow, wave some fucking wand.

I wouldn't have a clue where to start

looking, but. I mean maybe she's dead, too. Maybe everyone's dead.

I wish I was. Is there something wrong when your main ambition in life is to be dead? I don't think the people here would think that was a very good ambition. Every day when I wake up I don't want to get out of bed because I know it's going to take so much effort to stop from killing myself.

Oh yeah, did I tell you? I'm not in the Psych Ward any more. It's no big deal, some patients complained and then some high-up person said I wasn't allowed to be there because there was no security. That's what they reckon anyway.

It didn't matter, I don't care, it wasn't working out. I didn't co-operate with all their shit. It's no good for me. I don't deserve it.

When I left your house that terrible day, after doing that terrible thing, I nearly went to a shrink. I thought I'd find one and tell him what I'd done and then he'd sort of explain to me why it wasn't my fault, and he'd sort of look after me and stop the cops coming for me, or if they did come he'd stop them from hurting me. You know what I mean? I never did go to one, of course. Wouldn't have known where to start looking, but it wouldn't have helped anyway.

Instead of going to a shrink I ran as far and as fast as I could. God, I ran. I don't know how far I travelled. Million miles it felt like. I thought I was being chased or something. It would have been an hour before I stopped. Wish I'd been trying out for the Olympics or something, reckon I would have made it for sure. By the time I stopped I was a cot case. My legs wouldn't hold me up. Just buckled under me, got cramps or something. I felt all dizzy and my chest was killing me. I was down by the river, you know that bike path? I tried to walk along that a bit but my legs were useless and I ended up rolling down the hill, under some little bridge where they run the pipes across the river, I think it is. I got so thirsty I nearly drank from the river, but then I saw a tap along the way so I got water out of that.

I didn't know what to do, Miff. I knew I couldn't go to my uncle and aunt's and I knew I couldn't go back to school the next day. I knew I couldn't go back to school ever again. I couldn't think straight, to tell you the truth. I knew I was in deep shit but I didn't seem able to sit down and work it out. I actually went to sleep for a bit. When I woke up, geez, I was so stiff I could hardly move. My legs really hurt. Maybe they knew what was coming. It was about six o'clock and I was hungry as hell. I went down to a 7 Eleven, and tried that trick you taught me—you know, the two-for-one, where you take one of something to the counter and ask where the other size is, or the peppermint flavour, or the one with nuts, and after they show you and they're walking back to the counter, you put the first one in your pocket, and then you've got two.

Sure you've had to pay for one but you're still better off than if you paid for them both.

So I scored two packets of chocolate-chip cookies, one with hazelnuts, one without. I knew they were filling—I'd had them before. I had them for breakfast quite a lot when I was living with me dad. Then I went back down the river. I felt a bit better after I'd had something to eat. I started walking, didn't know where, just anywhere. I thought I'd better not go back home because my uncle would kill me if the cops had been there. If they'd found his dope plants, Christ, he would have killed me for sure.

So I walked and walked, or limped and limped, that'd be more like it. I was looking in people's windows, trying to see what was happening in the houses. Like, this house, the kids were being told to get to bed, and they were trying to get out of it, you could just tell that's what was happening. This place, the lady was talking on the phone. Next one was these young blokes, looked pretty wild, they were just getting into their first slab of the night, I reckon. I was trying to guess what goes on in people's houses, you know what I mean? Like, up front, everyone's so nice and la-di-da, oh yeah, we're such a happy little family, no problems here, no way. But when they go inside and shut the door, I reckon that's when the shit starts to fly. I reckon they're all fucked; never seen any that weren't. And there was one place I passed where they were having a full-on domestic, yelling and screaming. It made me feel sick. I just got the hell out of there.

After a while I started seeing things I knew, and I worked out where I was. It was them shops, Tozers and all them, in Carrington Road, I don't know what the suburb's called. 'Shit,' I thought, 'I did run a long way.' I stood in front of Retravision for a while, watching the TV. The news was on and I thought I might be on it but I didn't see nothing. Not as important as I thought I was.

I was trying to think where to go, and I couldn't think of anything much. Like, all my friends, I was thinking maybe I could crash their places, but I didn't know if I'd get them in trouble. Like, I knew I'd hurt your mum real bad and I knew it was serious this time, like I was really up the creek, I couldn't just rock up to a mate's place and say, 'G'day, thought I'd crash here for a few nights,' like I done lots of times when I'd had a fight with me old man or me uncle.

Then I thought maybe I could become a bum like the old alcos, and sleep in the parks and all that shit, but I thought 'Nah, too cold at nights, and them old blokes always look like they haven't had a shave or nothing, I don't want to look like that.'

Then I thought about the trains.

I was near Becker's Point by then, see, that big train station, with the interstates, and that's what made me think of it. I guess I was thinking about me dad, how he reckoned he'd shot through to Queensland and suddenly it seemed like a good idea. I had this feeling that if I could get up there to Queensland and just lie on the beaches in the sun and sleep and sleep—I was so fucking tired, I felt like I wanted to sleep forever—then everything'd be OK. I'd be in this, like, dream world, where no-one could get me and nothing'd go wrong.

That's the way I thought. Yeah, I know, you don't have to tell me: pretty fucking dumb for a bloke the school file reckoned was a genius or whatever they said.

So anyway, I went on down to the station and sussed it out. Fucking busy place, Miff, you ever been there? Wild. There's the country trains and the interstates, and the suburbans as well. Lots of people. I stood and watched them for a while. It makes you kind of excited seeing all these people coming and going on big trips, all their luggage and their food and their magazines, all these families doing stuff together. Must make you feel important, I reckon; like, for once in your life you're not just doing the same old stuff, going to school, going home, going to school, going down the shops, going home, going to school . . .

For once in your life you're doing something interesting and different, and fun even, maybe.

Watching them all, it made me get pretty fucking depressed though, I got to admit. I was just wishing I had parents who'd do stuff like that, just, you know, family stuff.

I knew I didn't have enough money to go to Queensland but I asked anyway. I got a shock when they said—I can't remember how much exactly but it was fucking expensive. Then I thought, 'Oh shit, I shouldn't have asked because if the cops come here looking for me they're going to know I'm heading for Queensland.' So that was a big mistake. But I still wanted to go there so I went and looked at the TV screens that give all the info. There wasn't no train to Queensland that I could see but there was one to Davis Harbour, and I knew that was in the right direction, and it was leaving in less than an hour.

It was Platform Four, I think, so I went up and the train was already there but there was hardly no-one on it. I watched for a while to see how it all worked but there didn't seem to be no big problem. No-one was checking the tickets or nothing. I'd already seen a few transit pigs but I wasn't worried about them because I knew they wouldn't be looking for me. They hate the cops and the cops hate them. So I thought, 'Well, fuck it, I'll just get on and worry about the problems when they come.'

I found a seat in the carriage that had the smallest number of people. I just sat there looking out the window at the tracks. They were pretty fucking boring and pretty fucking ugly. This train came rocking along, didn't stop, and I watched how fucking big and heavy it was. It wouldn't stop for nothing. Anyone got in its way, it'd be like, WHAM, wipe them right out, chuck them straight into nothing, in one split second.

Made me think, I guess.

There was about fifteen minutes before the train went and suddenly all these people were arriving and the carriage was filling up real fast. Made me a bit nervous. Then all of a sudden these two guards were standing there with a lady who had about six little bags. 'Could I see your ticket thanks, son?' the first guard said.

Well, I didn't know what to do. I thought it'd be too stupid to play the old checking your pockets and saying, 'Oh dear, I seem to have lost it, how careless of me' trick. So I sat there going red, then suddenly I thought of something and said, 'My dad's bringing it, he'll be here soon.'

But I'd left it too late, and I knew it sounded real weak, as soon as I said it.

'Well,' said the guard, 'you're sitting in this lady's reserved seat, you're in a first-class carriage, and you don't have a ticket. I think you'd better hop off.'

I was still burning red, I hate it when I do that, but I couldn't help myself, and I got up and walked out, feeling like a right fucking loser.

It was like being at your place, Miff. I'd gone into the rich people's world again, where I didn't belong, and right away they'd recognised that I shouldn't be there, and they'd kicked me out. I never belonged in your house, Miff, never fitted into your world. I was a trespasser. I really do think now that you used me as some kind of weapon against your mother. Like, I was the way you spat in her face. You weren't game to do it yourself, so you hired me to do it. Somehow I'm sure of that now.

Maybe I don't love you at all, Miff. Maybe I hate your fucking guts.

So anyway, there I was, standing on the platform, totally shitted off. I'd never even known there was such a thing as first class on trains until those turkeys busted me. Through the window of the carriage I could see them looking at me and one of them was talking on his mobile phone or walkie-talkie or whatever it was. I knew what was going on. I've been dealing with dickheads like them all my life. I started walking away quickly. They'd be talking to the transit pigs for sure, and now I was worried. The transit pigs are among the biggest examples of scum in this universe, but once they come after you they usually get you.

My heart wasn't in it, but. I felt sick. I was running away from them but where was I running to? It was a race with no finish line, no trophies. I think I started crying a bit even, just as I was walking along, but I wasn't going to let anyone see

that. I wiped the tears off, rubbed my eyes.
I didn't think about where I was for a little
time then I realised I was in the part where
the suburban trains come and go. I don't
know when I first thought of doing it.
A few people here, shrinks and all them,
asked me that. There's no answer. It just
sort of grew in my head like a bad flower. It
was the feeling that nothing good was ever
going to happen, nothing could ever get
better, I'd fucked the whole lot up. Every
last thing. I touched a rose and it died.
I had no fucking family who cared,
I couldn't go back to school, I couldn't get
no job even if I wanted one and, by
tomorrow, when they heard what I'd done,
I'd have lost all my mates. Most of all, I'd
lost you, Miff, the one thing, the one person
I totally relied on. I couldn't hack that, just
couldn't hack it. That's the trouble with
love. You got to lose it one day, everyone's
got to lose it sooner or later and, when you
do, it hurts so bad you just can't stand it,
you can't live any more. I was in this
cold–hot state. Cold, because all my feelings
had frozen, if I ever had any anyway. Hot,
because I knew I was going to walk onto a
railway platform and chuck myself under
a train and that'd fix everything up. I didn't
think of it as killing myself exactly, putting
an end to my life, just as stopping all these

problems. Stopping this bad bad hurting feeling that I couldn't stand no more. It was a cure. *The* cure. I was walking faster and faster. I just wanted to do it, get it over with. I knew if I stopped to think about it I'd get scared and chicken out, so I couldn't stop to think about it. Come on, Tony, keep walking. Here's a ramp. Lots of people, so there must be a train soon. This'll do, it'll do, it doesn't matter. Come on. Up the ramp. People everywhere, looking that tired and grey, like they'd lost interest in life. Like their lives were so dead. They looked sad. Crowds of them and not one of them saw me, never even looked at me. I didn't see one pair of eyes that were alive or laughing or taking any notice of anything. I felt like I was in a crowd of dead people already. I got to the top of the ramp, looked around, saw where the end of the platform was, went round the back of the crowd to the end, then moved through them to the edge. No-one touched me. I was kind of floating. I felt like I'd entered another world, where no-one could touch me any more. Don't ask me to explain it, Miff. I think I'd sort of died before I even got there. This blast of air started coming along the platform and there was this vibration starting, like 'the train is coming, the train is coming'. You could feel people stirring, getting ready, coming forward. No-one was more ready than me though, no-one. I was ready. I don't think any doubt entered my mind.

I was right up the end so the train'd still be going fast, it had to be going fast enough. I saw it coming, but I didn't really think of it as a train, just as something that I had to get in front of. Something I had to throw myself in front of, and then whatever was going to happen would happen. Simple really, no problems. I was waiting for it, ready to go, all tensed up, all ready, waiting for it.

And I fucked it up. Funny how you do some little thing slightly wrong and that's it then, it's a major fuck-up. I'm still not sure what happened. I think I thought that the train was slowing up too much, that it might end up going too slow to do the job. And also, I don't know, at the same time I didn't want to leave it too late. To miss the train. It was like both these things were happening in my head at the same time. So anyway, to cut a long story short I did it a bit early.

I took the step forward, just one step. It was the weirdest feeling, stepping into space, into nothing. I knew it was going to hurt, but I wasn't scared. I was still just thinking, 'This'll fix it all up, take care of

things. No more pain after this.' But maybe
as I landed I wimped out a bit, without
meaning to. I heard this chick scream
behind me as I went down, and I think that
put me off a bit, made me think maybe I
shouldn't have done it, maybe I'd done the
wrong thing. She sort of scared me. And so
I think I must have fallen backwards, sort
of made myself fall backwards, made myself
fall away from the train, because I was
scared of the impact. Fucking lot of weight
in a train. So my top half—well, a bit more
than half—was under the platform before
the train hit. It was all because I was a
second too early, see. If I hadn't gone early
the train would have hit me before that
happened, see. Would have hit me on the
way down. But that's what did happen,
that's what I figure anyway. And that's why
I didn't get killed, and that's why I just lost
my fucking legs, all the way up to my dick,
just about, plus fucked up my spine. And
that's why I'm in this fucking wheelchair.

Funny thing, Miff, after it happened and
they got me out I was still conscious, you
know, and there were a million people on
the platform by then, because I'd fucked up
their evenings good and proper, and they
were all going to be late home. Stupid, I
was trying to say sorry to them, but no-one
would have heard or had a clue what I was

on about. But you know something, Miff? Something strange? All them people, their eyes were alive now, and they all saw me. The cops had put up a barrier and they were all behind it, but they were looking at me and they saw me and their eyes were alive. And don't ask me what the fuck that means, Miff, because I just don't know.

But I think it means something.

Bye for now,

Tony

Dear fucking bastards who've been reading these letters. I know you've been reading them now. You cunts. I hope you've had a lot of good laughs. Been making copies, have you? Been taking notes? Well, fuck you all. That's the last time I write anything. Just so you bastards can read it. FUCKING MIND YOUR OWN FUCKING BUSINESS. FUCK YOU ALL.

Lots of love, fuckers,

Tony